THE GUIDE FOR A SINGLE MAN

THE GUIDE FOR A SINGLE MAN

AARON GOLDFARB

FG PRESS | BOULDER, COLORADO

The Guide for a Single Man
©2014 Aaron Goldfarb

All rights reserved. No part of this publication may be reproduced, stored, or transmitted in any form or by any means, electronic, mechanical, photocopying, recording, scanning, or otherwise, without written permission from the publisher. It is illegal to copy this book, post it to a website, or distribute it by any other means without permission.

ART DIRECTOR | Kevin Barrett Kane

EDITOR | Dave Heal

COVER PHOTOGRAPHER | Dane McDonald

COVER PHOTOGRAPH LOCATION
License No. 1, Liquor Bar
in the HOTEL BOULDERADO
2115 13th St.
Boulder, CO
WWW.LICENSE1BOULDERADO.COM

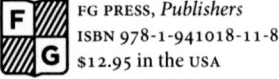

FG PRESS, *Publishers*
ISBN 978-1-941018-11-8
$12.95 in the USA

OTHER TITLES BY AARON GOLDFARB

The Guide for a Single Woman

How to Fail: The Self-Hurt Guide

The Cheat Sheet

Drunk Drinking

Inspired by Craig.

Facilitated by Phil.

Dedicated to Betsy.

TABLE OF CONTENTS

- 1   CHAPTER ONE
  Fuck Sex

- 10   CHAPTER TWO
  Why Shouldn't You Have Sex?

- 18   LESSON NUMBER ONE
  The Importance of the Porno Hook-up

- 25   CHAPTER THREE
  Why Don't You Want to "Get Lucky"?

- 33   CHAPTER FOUR
  Why is Being a Single Man Like Being On a Bar Crawl?

- 42   LESSON NUMBER TWO
  A Relationship Can Feel Like One Long Day

- 47   CHAPTER FIVE
  How Does a Woman's Age Affect Things?

- 55   LESSON NUMBER THREE
  The Dick and Pussy Insurers

- 62   CHAPTER SIX
  Why Could You Say of New York: "Bright Lights, Big Titties"?

- 72   CHAPTER SEVEN
  Whatever Happened to Job Security?

- 79   LESSON NUMBER FOUR
  There Is No Such Thing as "The One(s) Who Got Away"

- 87   CHAPTER EIGHT
  Why Do Some Men Think Being an Asshole to Women Makes Them an "Alpha Male"?

- 95   LESSON NUMBER FIVE
  Even Fat Asses Have Admirers

TABLE OF CONTENTS

CHAPTER NINE	**Why Don't Most Men Understand: SHE LIKES YOU!?**	101
LESSON NUMBER SIX	**A Man Can Learn From Chick Flicks**	109
CHAPTER TEN	**What Do Women Want?**	118
LESSON NUMBER SEVEN	**You Should You Never Lie to Women**	128
CHAPTER ELEVEN	**Why Should You Have as Much Sex as Humanly Possible?**	136
LESSON NUMBER EIGHT	**"To Do" Is More Important Than "I Do"**	141
CHAPTER TWELVE	**Why Do You Need to Sexually Graduate?**	149
CHAPTER THIRTEEN	**Why Does Fortune Favor the Bold, or At Least Assure He Gets Laid?**	155
CHAPTER FOURTEEN	**Should You Send Your Kids to The Machiavelli School for Children?**	163
LESSON NUMBER NINE	**You Need to Know What You're Looking For**	174
CHAPTER FIFTEEN	**Why is a Single Man's Life a Boozetrap?**	180
LESSON NUMBER TEN	**Devin's Final Lesson**	191

ABOUT THE GUIDES

The Guide for a Single Man is the first of its kind. Not a sequel, not a prequel, but an *equal*. Its counterpart is *The Guide for a Single Woman*. Two novels that can be read in either order or completely by themselves in order to learn the full story of two men and two women, and one night in New York.

THE MAP

- **Drunx Pub** (w. 52nd St. & Eleventh Ave.)
- **Valhalla** (w. 54th St. & Ninth Ave.)
- **Bar Nine** (w. 51st & Ninth Ave)
- **Gastro!** (w. 49th & Eighth Ave.)
- **Sven** (Columbus Circle)
- **Rudy's** (w. 44th St. & Ninth Ave.)
- **Bloopers** (w. 43rd St. & Eleventh Ave.)
- **Sandbar** (w. 49th & Tenth Ave.)
- **J. Mac's** (w. 57th & Eleventh Ave.)
- **The Horse-Around Bar** (W. 55th St. & Tenth Ave.)
- **Mario's Big Pie** (w. 54th & Ninth Ave.)
- **Flaming Saddles** (w. 53rd & Ninth Ave.)

"And when the lights came up at two,
I caught a glimpse of you…"

-Warren Zevon, "The French Inhaler"

chapter one

FUCK SEX

"Sex-ed really did a terrible job."

"Of what?"

"Of educating us. About sex."

"We were in sixth grade."

"So you remember?"

"Sort of."

"What was it? 1990?"

"OK. We were twelve."

"Yeah. I remember standing behind you in the boys' line. Nervously eyeing the girls beside us, like we were headed for the electric chair."

"I wasn't nervous."

"Of course you weren't, Devin. You always knew what to do with girls before any of us even knew what we could do with girls."

"I guess."

"That's just how it was. You really don't remember?"

I thought back to that sex-ed assembly. I recalled being split into separate groups. I guess they assumed the girls would be self-conscious when shown filmstrip fallopian tubes. That us boys would act immature upon learning what the pituitary gland actually does.

At that age, amongst the genders, you cannot make the pubic public.

So they threw us boys into the cafétorium where we did indeed laugh at illustrated ball sacks. Rolling around on the linoleum floor, shoving each other in manic glee, continually repeating the word "pubes."

Meanwhile, the girls were in the band room watching a '60s-era slide show that included hundreds of images of giant, erect penises. This was revealed later that day during lunch by Tricia Younger. She proudly noted to me that every girl had her mouth agape except her. Which was ironic as Tricia would quickly become the kind of girl who always gaped open her mouth for a giant, erect penis.

The boys assembly was run by a local gynecologist and amateur bodybuilder named Dr. Van Dyke. We quite obviously called him Dr. Veiny Dick.

"All y'all will soon learn, once you get a li'l older, ain't nothin' more beautiful than *coitus*!" he loudly proclaimed.

Coitus was a word we didn't know at the time, just like *fornication*, *intercourse*, and *fellatio*. Fancy words for what we yet didn't know were un-fancy acts. Still, after the assembly, we immediately circled all those words in the classroom *Webster's*.

The girls assembly was run by our dumpy school nurse, Miss Holmes. We quite obviously called her Miss Homo. Tricia giggled in reporting Miss Homo struggled to get through any sentence with the word copulate in it. We counted it up later: the McGraw Hill Sexual Health Instructor's Guide, Volume 15 (©1979) had 427 mentions of "copulate," "copulation," or "copulating" in it.

Though both assemblies were just an hour, we learned a lifetime of useless shit from Veiny Dick:

"Nocturnal emissions are nothing to lose sleep over."

"No, anal sex is not considered a legitimate expression of love."

"*Uhn-uh*, Justin Martin, you *cannot* use Saran Wrap as a prophylactic!"

It was the same useless shit boys and girls had been taught since the beginning of time. Or, at least since sex-ed assemblies became prominent in the public education system and class clowns like Justin Martin asked questions simply meant to make classmates laugh.

"So, yeah, I guess I remember that assembly," I told Les.

"Good. Because I would imagine everyone in America—except those home-schooled weirdos—remembers a similar sex-ed experience."

"It's part of 'growing up.'"

"That's my point!" Les lightly backhanded my shoulder.

"What's that?"

"That maybe it *shouldn't* be."

"You want to eliminate sex-ed?"

"I never said that."

"You just insinuated."

"I'm not some ultra-conservative creationist wackjob who believes dinosaurs helped Moses part the Red Sea."

It was almost shocking our shitty middle American school hadn't taught us that.

Les continued, "Look, Devin, what I'm simply saying is, they really need to change sex-ed. Make it more…realistic."

"And how would they do that?"

"By being more honest."

"No one's honest about sex."

"Exactly! And that's the problem. *The* point of sex-ed was never to teach us anything useful. It's never been to sexually educate children."

"OK. Then what was the point?"

"'The point,' Devin? The point was to scare children away from ever *fucking*!"

Les looked me in the eyes, dead seriously.

"And how do they do that?"

He counted with his fingers:

"By evoking religion,

 "with doomsday thoughts of pregnancy,

 "oh, and don't forget, frequently showing pictures of disgusting dick diseases."

He was kind of right. Back in 1990, Miss Homo preached to Tricia Younger and the other girls:

"Thou shalt not couple unless in love. And married. Under God. Jesus, too. It says so in the Bible. Genesis, I believe. Look it up, ladies. Minister Simpson says it's all there."

For some reason the separation of church and state has never seemed to matter if it keeps children from sticking their wieners into things or having wieners stuck into them.

At the same time Miss Homo was lying to the little girls, Veiny Dick was ranting to us boys:

"Babies having babies?! Now how ya gonna find a babysitter on prom night? You are the babysitter, bucko!"

After that line Justin Martin cracked a joke about losing *his* virginity to his babysitter and was immediately removed from the room. Of course, Justin was a father by our senior year and, as best as I can judge from Facebook, now has three children from two different women. He traded in "class clown" for "bartender at a Pizzeria Uno in the mall."

"Of course, we also had to watch never-ending slides"— CLICK, CLICK, CLICK—"of inflamed genitalia"—RED DICK, OOZING DICK, BUBBLING DICK.

"That flaming dick was seared into my brain."

"Still, it didn't work, Devin, did it? All that shit—religion, pregnancy, disgusting dick diseases—*didn't* work! Not for Justin Martin, not for Tricia Younger, not for you, and certainly not for me. You know why?"

"Why?"

"Because there's nothing we crave more than sex. Pregnancy, disease, and God be damned!"

"So…"

"So…what Homo and Veiny Dick should have said, if they truly wanted to deter us from sex, was something like: 'Don't have sex, kiddos, because: you'll *never* be able to get enough of it!'"

I knew where he was coming from. Like most men, my best friend Les had had his sexual highs and sexual lows. Those certain times women—or more likely, A (singular) woman—couldn't get enough of him, and those certain times when he was as hard up as a man could possibly be. Hard up with a hard-on. A terrible way to live one's life, I've always told him. Yet, he always told me, sadly, far too much about his sex life.

LESLEY MANN
Lifetime Statistics

SEXUAL DEBUT	May 25, 1996
TOTAL PARTNERS	11
TOTAL PERFORMANCES	328 (over 235 days)
LONGEST HOT STREAK	9 straight days (8/14–22/09)
LONGEST COLD STREAK	280 straight days (3/9–11/5/03)
LIFETIME AVERAGE	235 / 6,044 = 0.039
FRANCHISES	0

A guy his age could have done better in life. A guy his age should have done better by now. He had to know this. He continued ranting.

"'Don't have sex because, even though it's the most important thing in the world, you'll rarely get to participate in it!'"

For him, that was true. A mere 4% of his days since becoming sexually active had been days Les had actually *been* active. Assuming each act, foreplay to finish, generously averaged ten minutes long, then the most important thing in the world was something Les only got to participate in 0.00001% of his life.

"Even when the going's been good, Devin. Even when Jenn or Alice or *fucking* Katey couldn't get enough of me. Early on in our relationships of course. Even if she'd just had sex with me one hundred days in a row? That one-hundred-and-first day when she *didn't*, when she just rolled over and went to bed and I'd be left tossing and turning until I was finally forced to turn over and toss it? That always felt like the *worst* day of my life."

Women didn't realize how pathetic guys like Les could be. How getting a sexual advance rebuffed could absolutely crush their fragile male egos.

"Devin, why didn't Van Dyke just say: 'Don't ever have sex, boys, because it'll make you too self-conscious!'"

Les looked at me sadly.

"Especially when you're not having any. 'Why won't someone fuck me? Am I ugly? Getting fat? Do I smell? Am I too poor? Bad in bed?!' The best thing, I now realize, about me being in relationships, is that I lose all that shitty self-consciousness."

When Les was single, he was always obsessing over things. Constantly worrying about his male relatives who were bald (father, grandfather, two uncles) and how early they'd gone (19, 22, 21, 23), and being certain he too would be bald one day. The idiot used to waste $90 a month on Minoxidil, even though he had a head of hair thicker than the rough at Augusta National.

"Should I go back to the Rogaine? I wonder if that's why Jenn dumped me." Les tried to examine his hairline in the bar's dirty wall mirror. "Did I just become too relaxed in our relationship?"

"That's not why, Les."

Single men were so much sharper about the world around them. Most men's brains became mush when they were in a relationship. Jenn had turned Les's brain into mashed potatoes.

"If I ever get another girlfriend, I'm going to have to stay sharp, not become too relaxed, you know? I don't want a Jenn situation to ever happen again. 'Don't have sex, kids, because…'"

He paused.

"Because…?"

"Because…because…because. I got nothing."

Les slumped down on his barstool, completely spent.

"I can't stop thinking about Jenn. Three hours ago she was my girlfriend. Now she's just a memory." He exhaled. "'Don't have sex because: it'll dominate your thoughts.' 'Don't have sex because: you'll grow to hate yourself.' 'Don't have sex because: it'll make you screw over your friends just to screw all over some questionable girl you just met.'"

"What's that?"

Les lifted himself up and looked me in the eyes, apologetic.

"Devin, I have to apologize. I can't count the number of times over the years we'd be talking to the same girl and the second you went to take a leak, I swarmed on her."

Les shook his head in disgust at himself.

"It's OK, bud." I usually went to the bathroom simply to stick those women with Les.

"'Don't have sex because: it drives you to treat friends as rivals.'"

Les bent his head down toward his lap. Even though he'd only had a single beer, I was starting to get concerned he might yack.

"'Don't have sex, you little bastards, because: it'll make you physically ill.'"

He looked back up at me, his face turning pale.

"'Don't have sex because: you'll soon need it just to validate your pathetic existence.' I am so pathetic, Devin. So pathetic! If I had the chance, I know I'd fall to my knees like a sinner at the Pearly Gates, staring upward at a massive vagina consuming me, crying out, pleading: 'Please tell me I'm good, Saint Beaver! Please loooove me!!!!'"

I laughed, thinking Les was trying to be funny for once. He wasn't. A few bros at the end of the bar glanced over at Les's histrionics.

"I am so fucking pathetic. 'Don't have sex,' they should have said, 'because: it will…eventually…*ruin your life.*'"

Les was shaking. I put my hand on his back to steady him.

"I can just see myself later tonight, sitting in my empty apartment with a fifth of whatever, composing a note:"

> DEAR JENN'S VAGINA,
>
> I HAVE DECIDED TO KILL MYSELF BECAUSE YOU WILL NO LONGER FUCK ME...

I bit my tongue. Les could really be crazy sometimes.

"The misery that comes with being an adult in love. Is it even worth it?! I'm not so sure anymore."

"It *is*."

"Sometimes I envy eunuchs. My stupid dick has just led me like a divining rod toward a gold mine of misery."

"That's not true, bud."

"But it is! I was such a happy boy growing up. You know that! And, then, I wasn't. Because girls came into my life. Girls I wanted, but couldn't get. My mind told me I needed them, my body told me I had to have them, and every other force in the world conspired against me so I couldn't get them."

"Well, it's sometimes hard to be an adult looking for love."

"Or sex. That's all I'm saying, man. All Veiny Dick had to say to us was, 'Don't have sex…because it will totally ruin your fucking life.' Without getting a disease, or accidentally getting anyone pregnant, or even angering God, sex will still ruin your motherfucking life."

Les gripped my shoulders with both his hands, pulling me in close.

"It's ruined mine, Devin. *Fuck sex*. That's all they needed to teach us in sex-ed. *Fuck sex*. The assembly could have lasted just two minutes. *FUCK. Sex.*"

I didn't know what else to do but give him a hug. The bros

at the end of the bar watched closely. Les broke from my clutches and pulled back.

"But maybe I'm just saying this…because I'm pretty sure…I'm never going to get laid again."

📍 **Drunx Pub** (w. 52nd St. and Eleventh Ave.) | 6:35 PM

chapter two
WHY SHOULDN'T YOU HAVE SEX?

Les never called me on the phone, so when I'd seen his name flash on my iPhone screen I knew something was up. He wanted to go drinking with me. He never wanted to go drinking with me. Not anymore, at least. "Twist my liver," I'd responded, and now we sat at our once-favorite bar in Hell's Kitchen, Drunx. The post-work crowd continued filing in as I continued trying to cheer Les up.

"Come on. 'Don't have sex?' Don't be silly. 'Fuck sex?!' Fucking ridiculous!"

"Refute my points."

"Look, Les, there are almost no reasons not to have sex."

"There are plenty."

"I count…zero to five depending on your lack of morality and/or risk aversion."

Les thought about it as I continued.

"Yet, even you must realize there are zillions of reasons to have sex. Reasons that brought civilization to the place we currently sit and which continue to propel us forward. Plus…it's *way* fun."

"If it's so fun, why am I always so miserable?"

He wasn't going to listen to me. He simply wanted to complain tonight.

"Because you're not drinking fast enough."

I pushed the pint glass toward his face and he took a small sip. He stared at the cardboard box sitting on the bar top in front of us.

"This box she handed me was full of shit. Come to find out, so was she."

The box held all of Les's possessions that had migrated over to Jenn's apartment over the last two years.

"She was full of shit and lies, excuses and blow-offs. A few months ago, she was giving me blowjobs. Now, blow-offs."

"Easy come, easy go, right, bud? And from what you've told me, you never found it easy to make her come."

"I just hadn't seen it coming, Devin."

He was barely listening. He stared down at the filthy bar top, lacquered shiny from years of spilt BudMillerCoors, words carved into its slick wood. His eyes seemed to fixate on one carving in particular: "RED SUX BLOW."

"But when you saw Jenn coming, with a box full of your shit, even *then* did you see 'it' coming?"

"Actually, when I saw her coming through Times Square, emerging from a cloud of tourists lining up to see that shitty musical remake of *The Black Cauldron*, I thought to myself: 'Les, you have it pretty good.'"

"Did you really have it that good though?"

He turned toward me.

"Devin, I have a theory that life is a constant struggle to get everything going good at once. Like the faders on a recording studio soundboard, you know? When you raise one thing you have to lower something else to make it all work out. When I had great jobs, I was lonely. When I had great girlfriends, I was poor. When I had money, I had no social life."

Unsuccessful men always had dumb theories for why they were unsuccessful.

"But, for the last year, everything had been cranked to

eleven. Love, sex, work, friends, health. *Everything.*"

"Hey, even the Knicks have started winning."

"Yeah, well, J.R. still sucks a dick."

"At least someone does," I added, testing his limits. "Come on now, throw that fucking box in the trash."

"I can't."

It was a real eyesore sitting on top of the bar. It was doing us no favors in the "attracting women" department either.

"I had a beautiful girlfriend, Devin. Blonde, thin, smart. She was exactly one inch shorter than me when wearing her highest heels!"

"Forget her."

"This was usually our time. We always met Fridays after work, usually at an uptown wine bar. Certainly not a dump like this. Jenn and I have such rough work weeks, we like to kick the weekend off as soon as possible. 'TGIF-ASAP!' we always joked."

"Funny…"

"No it's not. There will be no TGIF-ASAP tonight."

"There can be. We haven't gone drinking in forever. Now let's tie one on tight." I slapped Les on the back. "It's happy hour. Be happy."

I wordlessly raised a two finger Victory sign as I made eye contact with our aloof bartender with decidedly unaloof tits. One-dollar bills covered the bar like a strip club stage, every idiot in here trying to tip their way into her tight pants. But, all these bros were too young to know George Washington was a shitty wingman.

"Happy hour is for amateurs. I'm leaving after this one."

It looked like Les was about to cry right in the middle of Drunx. It was quickly becoming sad hour. "Beers, half-price; tears, full-on."

"I thought I was so tough, Devin. I thought the only things that could make me cry occurred "out there" in an artificial reality. You know, movies about a dying old fart, reports about shitty education in the Third World, that ASPCA commercial with the Sarah McLaughlin song…but I'm just a real pussy aren't I?"

"Well…"

"I'm just a real fucking pussy about to burst into tears because a woman I've known for just about two years has implicitly told me I will no longer be allowed to buy her dinner, sleep in a bed with her, hang out with her lame family on boring holidays, see her naked, fuck her once a month…"

"Ouch. How did it end?"

Les looked at me.

"She asked for a hug! Do you believe that? A hug."

"Did you…?"

"Of course not! I yelled at her! 'You're dumping me and want a hug? Maybe I could buy you another pricey dinner too? Or some roses? Do I at least get the memory of one more roll in the memory foam?!'"

"You didn't say that."

"Maybe I did."

"You're a nice guy."

"Nice guys quickly become nasty assholes in times of peril."

"Then…?"

"Then…" he looked down, sheepishly. "I hugged her."

"It's OK."

"Then? She turned and walked away and I just watched like an idiot. I was certain she would turn back, but she didn't. Not even a glance. She just kept walking. Somewhere around 58th Street was the last I could see of her, right by that Thai restaurant with the punny name."

"Appe-Thai-zing?"

"I'm gonna unfriend her right now."

Les pulled out his Blackberry and began furiously tapping and scrolling.

"I wonder if Jenn is crying right now. I sure hope so."

"Probably. But girls cry over everything."

"I wonder what she'll do tonight."

"Order sushi, pet her stupid cat, get cheered up by her dumb roommate, watch *The Biggest Loser*."

He looked at me.

"I wonder when's the next time she'll have sex."

I paused.

"I'm certain it'll be before the I do."

I suddenly had nothing to say and Les knew it.

"Exactly. *Fuck sex*. Just like I said."

We sat in silence for a minute, simply taking in the scene. Drunx was on Eleventh Avenue next to an autobody shop for cabs, just across the street from a park where Latino kids played sandlot like it was still 1940, right up the block from where *The Daily Show* taped. The bar catered to just-out-of-college shitheads who simply wanted to get shitfaced. Les and I were probably too rich and certainly too old and debatably too sophisticated to still frequent Drunx, but it was good to have loyalties in one's life. Especially if those loyalties got you within close range of young women.

"Les, this bar is stocked with cheap pitchers and slutty young girls—"

"You don't know they're sluts."

"They could be."

"No. Fuck them all 'cause they won't fuck me."

"You're being a misogynist."

"That's rich coming from you."

Les leaned his chin on his sternum, staring at the red vinyl seat between his legs, examining a rusty spring exploding through the fabric mere inches from his balls. My eyes bolted toward the door as a group of women slightly too old for Drunx entered.

"Here's some women for you."

"Who?"

"That one in the sparkly top—"

"Her?!"

"Her" was built like a Division-II lineman with packed-on foundation and lipstick to the point of clowndom. She wore a shimmery top and a desperate look in her eyes as she manically scanned the room.

"Yes, *she* will have sex with you tonight, Les. I'm certain of it."

"Gross."

"It's a slumpbuster. Even an infield single counts as a hit. Come on, let's go talk to her and her friends."

I stood and tried to pull Les off his stool.

"I told you, I'm not interested in sex anymore. Especially with that 'slumpbuster.'"

"Congratulations then. You've discovered one of those zero to five reasons to actually say 'Fuck sex': woman too unattractive for your *lofty* standards."

"It's not like that and you know it."

"Hey, if you're nervous, I'll talk to the other three."

"Oh, what a friend! You mean you'll talk to her three hot friends while I handle the slumpbuster?! Wow. Thanks!"

I laughed.

"OK, I'll admit it, *I* just wanted an excuse to talk to them."

Les refused to budge, shaking his head at me with a look of incredulity.

"You know, it's always weird for me to see strange women and think: 'You don't know it yet, ladies, but in a few hours, *at least* one of you will be having sex with my friend Devin here.' Tonight? I'll put even odds on that little blondie."

I looked over toward her, briefly catching her eyes. Cute.

"That could work. Now come on."

"Be my guest. I'll hold back though. I've learned all sex is just a booby trap."

"And an assy trap and a pussy trap and, man, that's what's so great about it!"

"No, again, that's why 'Fuck sex.' Even if I somehow have sex with one of those girls tonight, she'll just ruin my life tomorrow. That's what they *should* teach in sixth grade."

"Les, today's sixth graders are getting laid more often and more *disgustingly* than either of us ever have. A sex-ed assembly nowadays would have the students teaching the teachers!"

I spun back around on my barstool, coming face to face

with the bartender's heaving cleavage as she placed two foamy pints in front of us.

"Well, I guess you have it all figured out, huh?"

"What's that?"

"You're the single man, Devin!"

"What's that supposed to mean?"

"It means fuck and run, fuck and run, fuck and run. No attachments, no miseries, no break-ups. No *bullshit*."

"Bullshit. You don't know the half of my life."

"I don't need to."

Les may have been angry, but he wasn't angry at me. He was angry at Jenn, angry at himself, angry at a world that had, he thought, long conspired against him and his dick.

"Relax."

"I hate when people tell me to relax! Like it's that easy. Maybe I should have tagged along to yoga with Jenn. I would have surely learned relaxation techniques there. I'd probably still have a girlfriend, too and thus be perfectly fucking relaxed!"

"We all get dumped."

"You don't."

"Les, if you are going to love, you are going to feel pain. The only way to get the highs of anything, is to also get the lows sometimes. Now quit acting like a little bitch and throw away that stupid fucking box."

Les hopped off his stool like the rusty spring had ejected him.

"You don't get the lows! You always get the highs...and have the stories to tell."

"Oh, you want stories?"

"I've heard your stories. Every fucking night of my life."

"You haven't heard *all* my stories."

"I don't need to hear all the awesome things you've done with women lately. It would just depress me even more."

"I'm not going to tell you about the awesome blowjob I got last night...I'm gonna tell you other stories."

"Like what?"

I gently put my hand on his drinking shoulder.

"Les, I was once like you."

"You were never like me. You were always the guy who knew what he wanted and got what he needed."

"That's not true. I was once like you."

Les clearly didn't know what I meant.

"*Clueless*. An impetuous horndog floating through life with pure charm. I used to fail with women as much as I succeeded. I used to fail a lot more than you."

"But you succeeded a lot more too."

"Out of pure luck."

Les perked up.

"Yes, I have been a single man almost my whole life. But that was on purpose. Guys like you, Les, are often single men too, but you don't choose to be single, you just accidentally are. Single between shifts of trying to have a girlfriend. But I've always chosen to be single."

Les looked over toward the slumpbuster and her three friends, thinking for a second before he turned back toward me.

"OK, fuck it. Go ahead. Tell me how to be a single man. Just like you, Devin. Tell me a story."

And so I did.

lesson number one

THE IMPORTANCE OF THE PORNO HOOK-UP

Les, I've been hesitant to ever tell you this one because it's as unbelievable as the plot of a porn.

But these things do happen. The pizza delivery man blown by a customer. The professor thrown on his desk by a coed. The criminal taken to town by a female guard. Then there was Annie and I.

She was the only single woman, and I was the only single man, at Keith and Shannon's first "adult" cocktail party. You remember that one?

Keith and Shannon were the first of us to get married and were soon on a path to doing all the checklist standards of society. Like winning participants in a scavenger hunt of boredom, they were first to find the good relationship, the good engagement, the good marriage. They found good jobs and got good and loaded. Unfortunately, Les, when you get loaded on money you quit getting loaded on booze and ever having any fun.

Now people may still call me childish, but it's much better than being "adultish." Much better than being any of the other party guests who looked like they were straight from Central Casting:

```
*White Male 28-42 - office friend, wears
pleated khakis, tasseled loafers,
button-down collared shirt with crisp
white undershirt, face shaved seconds
before leaving the house, tousled hair
(or wispy baldness), rarely curses,
drinks Amstel Light or a single glass
of blended scotch (on ice), has boring
anecdotes about "The Market."

*White Female 25-38 - wife of office
friend, mother of two to three two- to
three-year-olds (possibly twins), wears
Lily Pulitzer dresses and flats, far too
infrequently highlighted hair usually
up in a pony, mani-pedi chipping,
drinks white wine or red sangria,
laughs at significant other's boring
anecdotes, frequently calls home to
check on the sitter.
```

As the only singles at this party, Annie and I immediately became the centers of attention in this group of men crippled by society's mores and the women who still kind of loved them. The women who rarely left the house anymore without pushing a giant stroller, of course, wanted dirt on Annie's dating life.

"Dating any cute doctors?"

Meanwhile, these neutered men wanted to use me as their surrogate, living vicariously through my sex life.

"So…have you ever had…a *threesome*?"

Live *through* me, not like me. It didn't make sense then, and still doesn't today.

In a way, the adultish party guests treated Annie and me like members of a carnival freak show—the werewolf boy, the world's tiniest monk, the single person:

"Do you have to shave everyday?"

"How do you see over the pews?"

"You're really happy being…single?"

To them we were losing that adultish scavenger hunt by never finding anything: not love, not marriage, not kids, not a house with a mortgage.

"Is it hot in the summer?"

"Do you ever feel further from God?"

"Don't you want more *purpose* in life?!"

Annie was cute but plain, skinny but not sexy, and as a freshly minted med school grad, she was obviously quite boring. Years of studying, sitting in libraries, hands-washing, and scrubs-wearing do not create social dynamos. Then again, would you want a general practitioner who could work a room like Dean Martin?

She wore a pager on her belt and party guests, in attempts at "humor," tried to make jokes.

"What are you, a drug dealer in 1992?!"

"Uh, no, I'm on emergency call," she explained. "This beeper only, uh, comes into play should two other doctors fall ill tonight. But that never happens."

Eventually, the adults got bored with Annie like they'd gotten bored with me and soon they were back to discussing whether they should move to Westchester or the Jersey suburbs to start a family. (Let's be honest: "Where are the schools better?" is just an elegant way of saying: "Which schools have *fewer* students of color?")

In adultish party situations like these, the two singles are usually drawn to each other like magnets, especially if I'm one of those magnets. Unfortunately, I didn't think Annie was interested in me and I wasn't all that interested in her. She stood slumped in the corner, a wilting wallflower, uncomfortable in her own flawless skin, which she surely had a dermatologist friend give her the latest free samples for. Still, I tried my best to strike up a conversation.

"I notice you're not drinking."

As I said, I didn't think I had much interest in her. Sexually or romantically, as a friend, an acquaintance, conversation partner, networking contact, or even drinking buddy. I just had no one else to talk to.

"I'm, uhhhhh, technically not *allowed* to."

She was unsure where to put her hands, her eyes, the used toothpicks from the tiny crab cake appetizers we were munching on.

"Why not?"

"Well, um, I'm actually 'on the job.' Even though there's, uh, only like a 1% chance I'll have to work tonight, as I mentioned earlier."

"Personally, I prefer a society where everyone drinks on the job."

Our conversation hit a lull before it even started. It was like trying to work a speed bag that didn't return when you punched it. Annie had nothing to say, like she'd forgotten her lines. Nor did she seem interested in anything I had to offer and, I tell you, I was offering my best. So, I had no choice but to say something about the one thing she might actually know about.

"Are check-ups just a scam to make you pull out your checkbook?"

Back then I agreed with our buddy Stu who claimed you only needed to go to the doctor if you got AIDS or broke your leg.

"Well..."

"Be honest with me. I don't want the answer you're *supposed* to give in order to make money for your industry. I want the real answer: how often should a guy like me be going to the doctor?"

Annie looked me up and down, scrutinizing me rabbinically, like a piece of kosher meat.

"Well, you're young, healthy, robust-looking..."

Annie crinkled her nose for one final study.

"Assuming you feel fine, you don't need to go more than once a decade."

"I KNEW IT! What a scam!"

Aaron Goldfarb | 21

"Shhhh…" she smiled softly. "Don't blow up our spot."

I laughed, then quickly clammed up.

"Although, actually…I haven't felt *quite* 100%."

"Oh no?"

She actually looked concerned.

"I'm sorry if I'm out of line…but…"

Luckily, I'd drank enough at this point to have the balls to ask about, well, my balls.

"Before this party, while I was in the shower, I found something?"

"What?" She leaned in closer.

"I found…a ball bearing-sized bump in my ball bagging."

"Hmmm."

"I'm kinda scared. Could it be the big testicular C? Will I finally have to go to the doctor and blow tons of money on a co-pay?!"

She studied me silently for a second.

"Follow me," she finally replied coldly, like a principal chastising a misbehaving student. Annie marched off and I had no choice but to follow. She led me to Keith and Shannon's bedroom bathroom and locked the door.

"Drop your pants."

The outside party sounds immediately disappeared.

"Excuse me?"

"Drop. Your pants."

Free medical work was even better than free drinks. That was my first thought.

Annie plunged her left hand into my boxer briefs and rolled my right testis in her hand. The examination was clinical. You always wondered how doctors could look at dicks and assholes all day without cracking up, or being disgusted, but in that very moment I finally understood. My dick wasn't even a part of my body, I was now like a dead man looking down from heaven at his dick in someone else's hand.

"That's a minor varicocele."

"Is that…bad?!"

"Just a vein enlargement. You're fine. If it gets bigger or starts to hurt, see your doctor. *A* doctor."

I exhaled and life resumed. The volume on the soundtrack became un-muted. I again heard party guests laughing in the distance, no doubt recounting some humorous moment from some Bravo reality show featuring boring rich people who liked to yell at each other.

"Jesus, that's a relief. Thank you."

"No problem. It's my job."

Yet Annie's hand was still on my problem like she still had a job to do. I looked down and fully came alive in her hand. I looked back up into her eyes. She dove in for a kiss before descending downward.

It had gone from clinical to pornographic in mere seconds. An innocuous situation escalated to unexpected sordidness at the drop of a hat, as if chunkily scripted by a hack screenwriter. I hadn't said a single piece of dialogue that should have seduced her. Yet, we had gone from saying ummmms and uhhhhhs to ooooohs and ahhhhhs within seconds.

[And, Les, this surely could have been one of those zero to five reasons to say 'fuck sex': completely inappropriate venue.]

When Annie was finished, or rather I was, she stood back up at the sink, scrubbing to her elbows as if prepping for surgery.

"We better get back to the party."

Annie left, leaving me alone in the bathroom. I stared at myself in the mirror, confused by what had just occurred. I used a hand towel ("OURS") on my saliva-slathered dick and gargled some Scope.

I returned to the party and for the next five minutes stood in the corner alone, cluelessly slugging an Amstel Light like every other douche present. Annie mingled at the finger foods table, fingering some pita points, seemingly making a point to ignore me.

BEEP!BEEP!BEEP!

Everyone turned as Annie's pager blew up, fully knowing

what it meant.

"Shoot!"

Annie looked down at her screen, getting frantic.

"Shoot! Shoot!"

She quickly gathered her stuff—

"Freaking Joel!"

—and began going around the room, quickly saying "I'm sorry" and "goodbye" to everyone there.

I was the last person she encountered on her way out the door. She held out her hand professionally.

"*GOOD* to meet you, Devin."

She stared deeply into my eyes.

"I hope to *SEE* you *AGAIN*."

I thought I knew what she was hinting at, what words she was stressing and caps locking, and for what purpose, but it was hard to be sure. Annie left, and two minutes later I Irish goodbye'd the entire party.

Once outside I stood in front of Keith and Shannon's luxury high-rise scanning the early evening Upper East Side landscape. Young couples pushing strollers, old folks walking off their dinners.

But Annie was nowhere to be seen.

♀ Valhalla (W. 54th St. and Ninth Ave.) | 8:10 PM

chapter three

WHY DON'T YOU WANT TO "GET LUCKY"?

"I was *at* that party, Devin. With Carolyn."

"I know."

As we pissed side by side at the urinals, I could see Les trying to recall the evening. Perhaps he remembered him and the other adults discussing sonograms from Jenn Stone's recent visit to the OB/GYN ("It's the size of a blueberry!"). Or the darling monograms on Jack and Kirsten Higgins's wedding gifts. Or maybe even the state-of-the-art holograms used in CNN's Obama/McCain election coverage. But he didn't recall me and he certainly didn't recall Annie.

"It wasn't *that* boring."

"Not for me it wasn't, bud."

"We just assumed you'd gotten bored and stumbled outside for awhile."

We'd crawled a few blocks northeast to Valhalla, a Viking-themed spot that wasn't as lame as that sounds.

"What, you don't wash your hands?"

"Of course I do. *Before* I piss. I wouldn't want dirty hands touching this marvelous dick."

Les rolled his eyes at me as we exited the bathroom.

The interior of Valhalla was all wooden, accented by ornate carvings of Nordic shit. Heroic Vikings were said to have wanted to go to Valhalla when they die, while semi-heroic happy hour heroes liked to belly up to Valhalla's bar until they were pickled like a corpse. Valhalla had stiff drinks as well as several large TVs blaring the NBA playoffs. Eric the Red would have loved it here.

We slid into two seats at the bar, right next to two girls in matching server's uniforms, starched white Oxfords tucked into tight black skirts. They both loudly recounted their workday while anticipating their play weekend.

"That four-top was the worst."

"The worst. I still can't believe daddy makes us do this!"

I had no interest in engaging any of my five senses with these two. Unfortunately, I couldn't prevent it.

"We should totes go to the Meatpacking District tonight."

"Is that still cool?"

"Was it ever?"

They stunk strongly of magazine perfume samples. They probably tasted like watermelon Bubblicious. Touching them would have surely scalded my hand. And they looked like identical twins with their frizzy black manes cascading over pointy-chinned faces.

"Hey, I thought you said your stories *weren't* going to be about awesome situations you fell ass-backward into."

"It was more like I fell dick-forward. But that's not the point."

"All that matters is it ended with you getting laid. All your stories do."

"No it didn't."

"Come on."

"If we're being accurate, it ended with me in the bathroom getting blown like a gram of coke. But I didn't get laid."

"Semantics. All your stories end up with you coming."

"Not…*all* of them."

"Even so, your sex stories aren't exactly Aesop's Fables either."

"Oh no? I might call that last one 'The Boy Who Cried Woof,

Woof.'"

Les rolled his eyes.

"'The Tortoise and the Hairless Brazilian'?"

A slight grin came over his face.

"'The Foxy Chick and the Fermented Grapes'?"

He'd had enough.

"I get it! Sure, *sometimes* you tell stories about how you screwed up a chance of getting laid because you were so drunk."

"That's true."

"But you're still just telling it to make yourself look awesome. 'I drank sooooo much I passed out and threw up and shit my pants and screwed up my chances with a smoking hot girl. But I don't even care because I get laid so much that screwing up my chances with one hot girl is no big deal to me!'"

"May I retroactively say 'touché?' Still, I haven't told a story like that in years. I've changed. I'm in my thirties."

"Yet you still have the stories."

I glanced around the bar at the pockets of friends talking to each other, it still too early in the night for the haphazard intermingling to begin.

"OK, Devin, go on, tell me how awesome that night with Annie makes you."

"That's actually not the case. You see, until my porno hook-up with Annie, I'd never once thought to analyze my sex life."

"Someone should certainly be analyzing you, that's true."

"Les, I broke it down in my mind thousands of times, like a football coach studying game film, continually rewinding, replaying, and freeze-framing the events of that one night with Annie."

"You know what Lombardi said: 'Getting laid isn't everything. It's the *only* thing.'"

"I wondered: what exactly did I do that evening that I could keep doing in order to turn *every single night* into a porno hook-up?"

With my repeated mentions of "porno hook-up," the girls next to us perked their ears like dogs hearing a distant noise.

"So…what was it?"

"Nothing. There was *nothing* to learn from my porno hook-up."

"Nothing?"

"I had simply gotten lucky."

Valhalla's bartender, Darren, brought us two Sixpoints and Les paid for them. I was on friendly terms with Darren but that didn't mean snappier service or comped drinks. It meant average service for us and awful service for everyone who wasn't friends with him. Male bartenders could be so unfocused, unlike female ones who just clinically went about their jobs, emotionlessly filling orders, trying to crank out as much tip money as they could.

"Lucky?" asked Darren as annoyed drinkers tried to flag him down. He was going to get shitty tips tonight then blame the customers for not understanding the service industry because they'd never worked in it.

"Yes, lucky. But that's not something to be proud."

"Says the always-lucky guy."

"Not always. You see, my first porno hook-up taught me I'd actually been depending on luck my entire life. But, what I should have been focusing on was a strategy."

"Strategy? Like some sleazy weirdo?"

"Not at all. The most important thing you can achieve as a single man is reaching the point where you are no longer 'getting lucky.'"

"Yeah?" asked Darren as he slowly fetched a Stella for some yahoo who'd been waving his meaty paws like a mad man.

"Master yourself and life will be a lot easier. So will the women."

Les pondered that for a sec.

"Les, you have to start devising strategies so you can control your own destiny and never again have to say: 'Man, I sure got lucky tonight!'"

He clearly wasn't satisfied.

"I'm actually more interested in learning *why* you always get lucky. And I don't."

Les always craved simple explanations to his problems. That was actually his problem.

"There *isn't* an explanation. Luck is luck. Nothing more, nothing less.

"'Nothing, Les.' Exactly."

Darren cut in. "Perhaps we should be asking: is Devin's luck just luck, or does he do things that cause this luck to occur? Are lucky people lucky at getting lucky?"

Darren had spent too much of his life inside dark bars, and like a boy raised by wolves his mind had quit maturing correctly.

The JAPs continued to yap:

"Should we go to Tao tonight?"

"Why? It's Olive Garden for Chinese food."

"No, P.F. Chang's is Olive Garden for Chinese food."

Les put his hand on my shoulder as Darren walked off.

"Devin, I love you like a brother, but I hate your stories. I don't just not kiss and tell, I hate tales of kisses. Look, let's just watch the game and relax. I mean, the Knicks are actually winning a playoff game. After last year, who woulda thunk *that*?"

"No, we're not going to sit around as passive observers of life. Although…*watch*." I immediately turned toward the two JAPs. "Excuse me, which of you two is luckier?"

The best pick-up line was one that left your mouth without hesitation.

"*What*…do you mean?"

They feigned surprise that I had spoken to them.

"Like I said, which of you is luckier?"

Their guards remained up as they looked at each other.

"Is this a trick?"

"Do I look like a wizard?"

"Huh?"

"It's not a trick."

One of the girls smiled slyly. "Who *are* you?"

"I'm Devin Satyr." I extended my hand and got nothing in

return. "This is the point where you put your hand into mine, we move them up and down, and you tell me your legal names."

Realizing how silly they had been acting, the two finally dropped their bitch shields.

"Sharon."

"Carol. Uh…did you say your last name was 'satire'? Is that a joke?"

"Nobody's laughing." I handed my New York State driver's license to Carol.

"Six…*one*?"

It said I was 6'1" even though I was shorter than that. The DMV let you put whatever height you wanted, and once your card was laminated it was like you'd officially altered the truth. If only everything in life could become official simply by lying to an unfocused government employee.

"Do you know what a satyr is?" Les butted in.

"Huh?"

"S-A-T-Y-R. Google it."

I was glad Les had joined the conversation, but his angle was way off.

"Why?" Carol looked at me. "Are you one of those guys who makes up identities to meet women?"

"Not really. Anymore."

"Then how 'bout you just tell us what we'll find?" Sharon flirtily added.

Les smiled, thinking he was onto something. "Well, you see, according to Greek myths, satyrs were creatures who roamed the woods."

"Yeah?"

"…in search of sex…"

"Sex?"

"…sporting perpetual erections."

I cringed.

"Boners?!" asked Sharon, nearly choking on the toothpicked row of martini olives she'd been eating. Carol stared at my crotch. Les continued.

"Yup. Satyr. Isn't that preposterous? It's like:
"The librarian named Bookman.
"The weatherman named Raines.
"The electrician named Watts…"

Sharon jumped in, finally understanding.

"We know a bartender on Long Island..."

The two looked at each other giggling: "Joey Corona!"

"Exactly! That's called nominative determinism." He was getting excited. "It was a deeply held belief in the ancient world. The belief that the name one was born with would lead to the life he would live."

Les was such a fucking nerd. I needed to save him.

"So what are your last names?" I asked.

"Stein."

"Goldman."

Les thought for a second.

"So a drunk and a gold-digger!" I blurted out. Now it was Les's turn to cringe, but the girls immediately ate it up.

"*Totally.* Have you guys been to Oktoberfest? We went to Munich last year."

"We must have had a dozen steins. Sooooo fun."

Carol and Sharon laughed in remembrance, before turning back toward us.

"What are you guys up to tonight? Happy hour or something?"

"Les and I are on a bar crawl right now."

"A bar crawl? Fun. Like, for *what*?"

"To honor this guy." I slapped Les on the back.

"For what?" they both asked, but I ignored them and pointed toward the TV. "Whoops, first quarter's over, we have to leave."

I snatched Sharon's Droid off the bar and quickly punched Les's number into it.

"Text this when you want to join up with us. Plenty of emoticons please." I playfully winked at her.

I threw back the rest of my beer and stood. I nodded toward the bar and Les threw down a few two-dollar bills for Darren's tip.

After following me out the door, we stood on the Ninth Avenue sidewalk. I could see Les was confused.

"What was that?"

"Just a little fun."

"They wanted to hang with us. Like right now."

"So now we've forced the issue. That's how you go from depending on luck to using a strategy."

"Won't it be luck if they actually contacted us after that stupid maneuver?"

"It would be even luckier if we kept them entertained from now until bedtime."

Les thought about it for a second and had to agree. I started walking south and Les followed like a stray dog.

"By the way, whatever happened with Annie?"

"That was it. I never saw or heard from her again. But she certainly changed my life more than just about any girl I've ever known."

Just then, Les's Blackberry buzzed and, surprised, he pulled it from his pocket:

> lucky running into u guys. where's next on the crawl? ;) – Sharon

◉ Bar Nine (w. 51ˢᵗ St. and Ninth Ave.) | 9:10 PM

chapter four

WHY IS BEING A SINGLE MAN LIKE BEING ON A CONSTANT BAR CRAWL?

"It worked!"

"Did it?"

"When should I text her back? Now? Or do I wait…?"

I snatched Les's phone put it in my pocket.

"A little strategy is good. Thinking too much isn't."

Les's dopamine levels, boosted from the cheap thrill of getting Sharon's number, dropped once again. I nodded at an industrial metal facade with an entranceway obscured by construction scaffolding. The tinted windows obscured everything inside but the bar's name, silk-screened onto the glass. Les snarked at me.

"I try not to go into bars with stupid names."

Ignoring him, I opened the wooden door, revealing a massive goon in a Rochester Big & Tall suit, propped up on a tiny stool.

"Welcome to Bar Nine, fellas. IDs please…"

The man paused the dumb game on his smartphone and examined our licenses using the glow of his screen.

"Think about it, Devin. Every man alive dreams of quitting his stupid day job to open a bar. We imagine what it'll look like, what'll be in it, what it'll serve. And some of us out there actually save up our money, take out bank loans with bad rates, go through the whole rigmarole of getting licenses with this corrupt city, and truly decide to gamble away our future on patronage from a bunch of drunks like us. But the owner here, when friends excitedly ask, 'What's that new bar of yours called?' has to answer: 'Bar Nine.' 'Why?' 'Well, it's on…Ninth Avenue.' Durrr."

The bouncer looked at Les, displeased, as he handed back his ID. "More clever than your name. *Mr. Mann.*"

I tried to smooth things over with the bouncer. "It is." I looked back toward Les. "You'll be glad we came here, bud."

Nevertheless, Les was kind of right. Bar Nine was trite, an extremely dark lounge that attracted clientele with faces that merited being in extremely dark lounges. It felt like walking into an amusement park haunted house, the imminent threat of some drama school dropout in a bed sheet about to pop out from a corner and say "Boo!"

I headed toward the bar.

"What do you want?"

"Water."

"With…?"

"I'm already too buzzed."

"Yes, that means it's *working*. Get a cocktail."

"Sure. Two jiggers of hydrogen, one of oxygen. Shaken not stirred."

"Quit being so lame. You know, you've turned into a light-weight and the worst kind too. A former heavyweight now lighter because of a shitty relationship."

I stared at him with disappointment until he finally relented.

"Fine, gimme…whatever."

Les handed me a stack of two-dollar bills and I slid between a pack of people desperately holding out paper like they were trying to buy stocks on the Exchange floor. I caught the eyes of a ginger bartender I kind of knew and called out to her:

"Two Redbreasts!"

"Whiskey? I can't, Devin. I've been drinking beer all night."

"'All night'? You've had two."

"Still."

"You actually follow the 'Beer before liquor' rule?"

"Of course I do."

Of course, Les was the kind of guy who followed the rules, even the ones he disagreed with. From an early age, adults had made him scared of breaking rules and therefore rules were something he never questioned. He didn't jaywalk, didn't smoke weed, didn't lie, cheat, steal, or, yes, drink beer before liquor.

In fact, Les was such a rules-following stickler, he hadn't even had a beer until he turned twenty-one.

"Remember your 21st?"

Les looked at me and his eyes lit up.

"My birthday? Of course."

"What'd you say after your first sip of Beast? 'I am doubtful…'"

"'…this is the finest brew Wisconsin has to offer.'" We laughed.

By his sixth can of Milwaukee's Best, and two additional vodka shots, he was throwing up all over our basement floor.

"I never told you…"

"What?"

He smiled mischievously.

"I lost my virginity that night."

"No, you lost your virginity on prom night."

"I didn't."

"You lied about Emily Zalicky?"

"Of course I did. Who, except a movie character, gets laid on prom night?"

"I did."

"Well…you're a character."

"But on your 21st? Who could possibly…? I've never seen someone throw up so much."

Aaron Goldfarb | 35

"Kaitlin Adamson."

"She was cute!"

"She was *way* into birthdays."

"Must have been. You smelled like a porta-potty."

Les's projectile vomiting had cleared out that party quicker than shouting "Fire!" in a crowded theater. Kaitlin had stayed behind to take care of him after everyone else headed out to the bars.

"Well…I guess she really wanted to blow out your candle."

The bartender handed us our Irish whiskeys. Les placed his traveling knick-knacks box on the floor between his feet as I passed him his rocks glass.

"Then that completely changes your sexual statistics."

"Huh?"

"You were wrong…you *do* have good luck."

"Kaitlin was a friend. It doesn't count."

"It always counts. Cheers."

I lifted my Redbreast toward his.

"I really don't want to drink any more."

"What'd I say about being lame?"

"What's so great about drinking?"

"Let's see, Les…camaraderie like we're currently having, happiness like we'll have after a few more, and helping us get laid which we hope to ultimately achieve. Which we both *will* achieve."

"There's many more bad things: weight gain, poor decisions, hangovers. *The Hangover*. High-fives, one-night stands, tequila shots, whiskey dicks."

"Drinking gives you a boost in confidence and a feeling of invincibility around women. It's 5-Hour Fuckergy."

"5-Hour Lethargy. I'm ready for bed."

Les yawned. Drama queen.

"And I hate bar crawls more than anything."

Loud hip-hop music wailed from warbling speakers. The Knicks game headed to halftime with them up five on the Hawks.

"We're at our third spot of the evening. Not exactly a 'bar crawl.'"

"It's about to be. I know where this night's headed if I let you head me there."

"You just can't avoid bar crawls in New York."

"Why does no one hang in their apartment in New York? I have a nice place. Instead, life completely takes place in public. The deli is your kitchen, the restaurant your dining room, the park your backyard, and the bar your living room full of a bunch of people you hate. Bar crawls are the mindless channel surfing of nightlife."

"I need that novelty. I hate sitting still at one place.

"I was enjoying Valhalla."

"Fuck Valhalla! There's more women *here*."

"We *already* met women at Valhalla!"

"Then we'll meet more here. Up our odds."

"Odds are 100% you're ending the night with someone, I know."

"And so are you, Les!"

I looked him in the eyes and all of the sudden it was as if a switch had been flipped.

"Up my odds, huh? Then gimme back my phone, Devin."

I slowly handed Les his Blackberry, unsure what he wanted to do with it. Leaving his stupid box behind on the floor, he pushed the conversation-scrums in our immediate vicinity to the side and began walking toward the back of the bar.

"Let's explore," he called out.

"See … one … like?" I shouted in Les's ear.

"…"

I couldn't hear him, but I'm not sure I wanted to anymore. He was suddenly in a dark spot in this very loud place.

"Do. You. See—"

"…"

"WHAT?!"

"…"

Giving up on talking, I nodded toward a thin girl sucking

Aaron Goldfarb | 37

a vodka tonic through a thin red straw. The drink glowed turquoise under the bar's black light, yet her face was still hard to see. Les marched over to her.

She smiled nervously. The black light made her teeth appear purple and wooden, like a psychedelic George Washington. Les pulled out his Blackberry, turned on the camera's light, and held it above the girl's head, shining it on her face like a spotlight. She was a redhead with mild acne scarring. Les's tough guy facade instantly faded and he turned back to me. I was dying laughing at him, though I didn't want to discourage his newfound aggressiveness.

"Think of that as a trial run. Do it again."

I shoved him toward two slinky things standing side by side, looking around the bar. He now lit up their faces. They were attractive, angular with sharp, skeletal cheekbones.

"What. Are. You. DOIN'?!"

"I wanted to see what you looked like," Les boldly noted. "To know whether I have it in me to put it in you."

The girls looked stunned, but no more than I was.

Les rhythmically panned his phone back and forth on them like a rotating spotlight. I was dying.

"Do you feel like movie stars?"

They scoffed and turned away.

"Get that out of our fuckin' faces, creep."

Laughing even harder, I again pulled Les away.

"I don't think they felt like movie stars, bud."

"WRONG. That one chick probably feels like Steve Buscemi quite often."

Les actually appeared to be enjoying himself for the first time all night so I wasn't going to discourage it. I guess he was learning that he enjoyed acting like an asshole. He led us toward the darker back recesses of the bar. We brushed by the sweatiest dance circle I've seen since the last time I'd attended a Jewish wedding to get to a group of women in the corner. Each had a massive designer purse on one shoulder, sipping pink, red, and orange cocktails that seemed to tie each of their outfits together.

Les thrust his arm in the air above them all. I joined him from the other side, our phones illuminating the entire circle as Les plunged his head into it inquisitively, like Peyton Manning calling a play.

"So who's the hottest here?!"

"Who do you think you are?"

"I'm Mr. Mann."

"Well you're an fuckin' asshole!"

"No! I'm a...*nice* guy."

Right then a bloated paw reached in and yanked him and me from the circle with a vicious force. The two movie stars stood behind the beefy bouncer's love handle barricade, their hands on their hips and snarls on their faces. Holding us by the scruffs of our necks like little kittens, the bouncer marched us toward the front door, chest-passing us like two basketballs onto the sidewalk.

"I don't wanna ever see you two back at BAR FUCKIN' NINE!"

Crumpled on the sidewalk, I laughed at Les just as his knick-knacks box came hurtling toward us, its contents spilling out all over Ninth Avenue.

"86'd. The ol' heave-ho. Booted. Tossed. Eeeee-*jected*..." a nearby bum spoke in a Marv Albert voice as he began picking up Les's shit.

Les dusted himself off, grabbed his box from the homeless man, and handed him a crumpled two-dollar bill.

"See? I don't have to follow all the rules."

"Good work."

"Is it?"

He began marching away, looking angered. I hurried to catch up to him.

"I don't like to get in trouble, Devin."

"Oooh...*in trouble*. Ugly chicks turned down you down and a pituitary case tossed you from a bar you already hated. If I didn't know better I would have thought you orchestrated the whole thing."

Les turned back to lob a few verbal jabs toward the bouncer.

"Actually, that did feel pretty good."

"See?"

"And now I don't feel like having just one more. I feel like having *many* more."

"That's what I'm talking about."

He finally dropped his tough guy facade.

"Just please, some place…less terrible."

We began meandering south.

"Being single is like being on a constant bar crawl," Les noted.

"You think?"

"I do. Because just like bars, some women are loud and some are peaceful…"

"Then there are ones you can really think around while others you simply enjoy for the emotions you experience."

"Or the physical sensations you feel being inside of them!"

"Some are cavernous, some a tight fit. And, very few are just the right temperature."

"Most are just overly hot and sticky, huh?"

"Yes, I believe you're right."

"The fact of the matter is, Devin…most bars suck and so do most women."

"Sucky bars full of sucky woman. Who will perhaps sucky you tonight."

"One-night stands just don't happen to me."

"What about Kaitlin on your birthday?"

"Even that wasn't one. Though it should have been."

"What happened?"

"Instead of just letting it be, I actually began *courting* her. Although it was closer to stalking than courting."

"Fine line."

"I'd never had romantic interest in her before, but the second we had drunken sex I was 'in love.'"

"Happens to the best of us when we're young."

"I'd already gotten the milk without buying the cow and

now I was trying to go back and pay the stupid farmer. Luckily, Kaitlin knew that sometimes a one-night stand is just a one-night stand."

"And…?"

"She did have sex with me a second time. Just a pity lay, probably. So I would shut the fuck up and quit stalking her, but that was that. And that's informed the rest of my life."

"It doesn't have to. I can teach an old drunk new tricks."

"But I could never be like you. With me, Devin, it seems like the rare girl I meet who actually likes me wants to go from zero to committed dating as quickly as possible."

"You do give off that vibe."

"In fact, sometimes it feels like my relationships are just one long day. They go by that quick. I'm drunk, though—does that even make sense?"

"It does." I smiled. "Because my marriage lasted just one long day."

lesson number two

A RELATIONSHIP CAN FEEL LIKE ONE LONG DAY

Gretchen and I had lived in the same walk-up for a year, so we'd probably passed each other dozens of times in the stairwell without even realizing it. We'd surely drank in the same local bars at the same time, eaten in the same restaurants just tables away from each other, gotten burnt coffee at that same crummy bodega. But August 14, 2008 was our day to actually "meet."

The sun had just risen and so had I, holding Buster's leash as he took a crap on Riverside Drive. Ten feet away, Gretchen did likewise with her pooch Julio. After our dogs had finished, we both simultaneously reached into our pockets for a bag. Unfortunately, I had on mesh shorts and she had on yoga pants and neither of us had pockets so we both came up empty. In our sleepy hazes we'd forgotten to bring anything along, so we were each forced to look around for something on the ground, or in the nearby trash can. And, we kept looking around…until, our eyes met.

We laughed at our similar circumstances. Dog poop bringing people together like it's done for thousands of years.

Now, this wasn't exactly one of those dumb "meet cutes" they have in the movies—you know, Leo saving Kate from committing suicide off the Titanic—it was just two out of the seven billion people on planet earth coming into random contact with each other.

Gretchen held her finger to her lips—shhhh.

And Riverside Drive became Rivershit Drive as we both sprinted from the scene of the crime.

We kept running all the way to Amsterdam Avenue and coincidentally found ourselves in front of Sarabeth's, a brunch spot. Why not, we thought? And there, the Bonnie & Clyde of letting their dogs shit on the street without cleaning it up dined together at this sidewalk cafe.

Gretchen instantly found me witty and intelligent.

I instantly found her...to be in possession of a vagina. Sadly, that's often enough to create love at first sight for most men.

We chatted, ate French toast, and swilled bottomless Bloody Marys. We would soon be topless and bottomless.

Around us, people rushed to work. We both called in to our offices.

Gretchen: "I need to use a sick day, I think I may be coming down with something." ("You mean, going down on someone," I thought.)

Me: "I need to use a personal day." ("To get personal with someone.")

We tipsily sprinted back to our apartment building, choosing my studio since it was on a lower floor. Gretchen told me she had always played by those dumb rules *Cosmo* and *Elle* and *CityGirl* had about waiting "X" number of days to "F" the guy to assure he respected you. But she didn't want respect from me at that moment in time.

We ripped each other's clothes off and, just an hour after meeting, we were having sex. Unable to control ourselves. Our dogs sat in the corner carefully sniffing each other's crotches, far more respectful of the fact that they were essentially strangers.

From 10:30 to 11:30 AM, every fifteen minutes, as soon as my refractory period was over, Gretchen and I were fucking. Anywhere and everywhere. In the kitchen, the closet, the hallway, bathroom, and finally the shower in her apartment.

Damp from shower sex, we lay in her canopy bed, wrapped

in bathrobes, exhausted. We drunk dialed our respective friends at their respective offices.

"Stacy! You won't believe this." Gretchen turned and covered her mouth so I couldn't hear. "I just met this guy who I think is…'The One.'"

By noon, it was quite evident our time together was not ending any time soon. We joked that our relationship had already reached quote-unquote "official" status. We toasted with some champagne I still had lying around from a New Year's party.

We decided to get even more whimsical. Got dressed up, left our dogs behind, and went to the Atlantic Grill for lunch. We were famished from all the sex. We brought my iPad and loudly video-chatted with each other's parents on Skype. It was already 1:00 PM, so we figured it was time to meet the parents. It sure was funny to see the looks on my mom's face.

We switched to gin and tonics. We must have been totally plastered. We must have been making a ton of noise. The maitre d' politely asked us to leave. I politely asked him not to talk that way to my fiancée.

Gretchen giggled. "Yeah, and don't talk to my fiancé like that either!"

I snatched a napkin ring and put it on her finger.

"Where to now?" she asked.

"City Hall. Let's make it official."

We hailed a cab downtown.

Afterward, the new Mrs. Satyr and I walked to Battery Park City and boarded the Staten Island Ferry just as it left the dock. Our honeymoon! We were so madly in love.

I ripped off my stupid tie and threw it into the Hudson. Gretchen shook out her up-do. We felt like we had just pulled off a bank heist.

But, by 3:30 PM, as the ferry reached Staten Island, we were having our first fight. At the front of the ferry, yelling our brains out at each other. I'm not even sure if we were mad at each other. We'd probably just seen a bunch of sitcoms and knew that couples were supposed to fight. Or maybe we were just way too drunk at this point.

On the ferry ride back to Manhattan we moved to the top deck and chugged cheap canned beers while cuddling on the rails. Back in the city, now exhausted, we grabbed some sushi to take back to Gretchen's apartment.

We sat in her living room eating Haru. We'd already had such a crazy, tiring, *drunken* day and this felt comfortable. By now our friends were getting off work and heading to happy hour, finally returning our calls and texts to see what the fuck was going on. But we didn't answer any calls, didn't return any texts. We didn't want to go out. We didn't want to paint the town red, we didn't want to paint the town any color. We didn't even want to put shoes back on.

We were even sexed out.

We clinically rubbed each other's tired feet as we watched some mindless reality television. Our loving eyes were no longer on each other, but instead on *The Bachelor*.

Gretchen gazed at the dashing global financier on screen, surely wondering if she truly wanted to be with me for the rest of time.

I gazed at the twenty-five hot female contestants, thinking perhaps I'd prefer being with a brunette for eternity instead of my new blonde wife.

Soon, we had slowly migrated back to Gretchen's bedroom for our first night's sleep together.

By midnight, she was conked out and I was beside her, staring at the girl I was so madly in love with just earlier in the day. For the first time all day, she actually did feel like a stranger.

The next morning, sober again as I walked Buster, I realized why Gretchen felt like a stranger. Because she was.

Gretchen wasn't the person I thought she was, and I wasn't who she thought.

She wasn't the love of my life. And I wasn't her The One.

She shouldn't have been my wife. And I shouldn't have been her husband.

The previous day had been incredible, but this would all never work out.

We called in sick again so we could head back to City Hall and get our marriage annulled. I had the worst hangover of my life.

📍 **Gastro!** (W. 49th St. and Eighth Ave.) | 9:50 PM

chapter five
HOW DOES A WOMAN'S AGE AFFECT THINGS?

"My relationship with Jenn feels like it started this morning. Now it's over. What a waste."

"A relationship is never a waste if you learn from it."

"So what did you learn from your sham marriage?"

"Uh…always carry around an empty bag for dog shit?"

I looked around Gastro!, a cheesy chain originating out of Columbia, Missouri that had just opened its first New York City location. It was a Midwesterner's idea of what a cool Manhattan gastropub might look like. It had exposed brick that was actually made of plastic, granite bar tops actually made of linoleum, and a "farm to table" menu that had surely neglected to mention a few steps in between. Factory farm to freeze-dried bag to eighteen-wheeler to Memphis distribution center to walk-in freezer to industrial microwave to, yes, our wood-laminated communal table.

"You have to give me something better than that. What did you really learn?"

"Don't make life-altering decisions drunk."

"I'll keep that in mind. Why'd you never tell me you were married?"

"You never told me *when* you lost your virginity. At least *I* left a voicemail."

"You know I hate talking on the phone."

"It doesn't matter."

"Marriage always matters. What happened to her?"

"Gretchen? I still run into her on occasion. Walking her dog. We never say shit."

"No pun intended."

"Huh?"

"Never mind."

"She has some new dork she's engaged to."

"I wonder if she's told him."

"Doubt it."

"Yeah, you're not exactly 'marriage material.'"

I laughed. It was impossible to take Gastro! seriously, and not just because its name forced you to feign excitement every time you mentioned it. Gastro! attracted a clientele who didn't quite have the balls to cross Eighth Avenue into Hell's Kitchen. The franchisee of this particular location was a client of Les's, so he insisted we check it out briefly. At least we could watch the final minutes of the Knicks' Game 1 victory.

"Then again, Devin, I'm beginning to wonder if I am either. Seriously, who am I supposed to find now?"

The comped alcohol was starting to get to Les, mixing poorly with the bar's overly bright lighting scheme. Les squinted his eyes as he looked at the bar's clientele: tourists post-dinner, business travelers drinking alone, and Times Square office workers still hanging onto a happy hour that had started hours earlier and which by now, now that most of their co-workers had headed back to New Jersey, didn't seem all that happy anymore. This place was awful. It would do magnificently.

"You need a younger woman. Check out those girls over there."

At the other end of the bar, a small group drank oversized pilsner glasses of Blue Moon with wilted orange slices. They looked like contestants in a beauty pageant, and not one you'd heard of. Their blonde hair poofed out like futuristic cycling helmets and their real breasts were firmer than the best fakes the Park Avenue cosmetic surgery community had to offer.

"What would I get from a younger woman that I couldn't get from Jenn?"

"Seriously? Look at those chicks."

"I see 'em. They look like contestants from a Miss 1980s pageant."

"True enough, but take off their Kelly Bundy miniskirts… and you'd see something spectacular."

"I'd rather take off those pounds of hairspray and layers of makeup. We were young once, but I don't sure remember young girls being all that great."

"You don't?! Young girls have tight bodies and thin faces, even though they eat like shit. Fast food, scooped bagels, and Tasty D. Even though they drink every night. And they don't like spending nights in, unless they're hungover or broke, but they're so easy to maintain. You don't need to wine and dine 'em; brewed and screwed is perfectly acceptable. Pitchers of cheap beer or well vodka, some shared spinach artichoke dip for dinner, then the 6 train home to fuck all night."

"Young girls are clueless in bed."

"Uhn-uh. Young girls can *fuck*. They don't yet have any misgivings about their bodies, so no position is off limits. She'll jump on top of you in reverse cowgirl, no fear you're staring at some imperfections on her ass. Why? Because there are none. She'll let you bend back her legs until she's kissing her kneecaps. Shit, she'll even let you fuck her in the shower. With the lights *on*! A young girl's like your own personal porn star. And not just because her education is lacking."

"OK. But there has to be cons."

"Sure. You'll be annoyed when she sleeps in on Saturdays, so bring reading materials along if you're staying at her messy place. All she'll have lying around are copies of *Us Weekly* and college textbooks she never sold back. You'll quickly shed your boredom, though, when she finally wakes up around noon and instantly wants to begin fucking again, every half hour 'til nightfall."

I looked him in the eyes.

"Les, with a young girl you'd get to be her sex mentor. Young girls have usually only had boys before, so even if you bring your "C" game you'll still make her come ferociously. She didn't even know she *could* orgasm she'll tell you proudly."

"And she won't with me either."

"She will. Because you'll constantly find excuses to make fun of her age ('Were you really two when Kurt Cobain died?!') and it will turn her on. She'll likewise find ways to make fun of *your* age ('Class of '96?! Like *high school* class of '96?!') and lingo ('Why do you still say "awesome," old man?'). You won't really care, though, because she's the one fucking an awesome old man."

"She's probably fucking kids her own age too."

"Of course she is, which is why you don't need to worry she's falling for you. That would be pure hubris. And, for the love of god, wear a condom, even if she claims she's on birth control. Young girls are forgetful and sometimes too dumb to remember whether to go clockwise or counter on their little pill container."

Les shook his head at me.

"Don't worry, you'll never have 'the talk.' You'll just understand where things are headed, and after a few months drift apart. She'll still text you on occasion, when she's really drunk and notices your name in her contact list, but you'll rarely respond. You'll casually follow along on Facebook as she lives her life, posting new going-out pics every Monday morning from her work computer, getting in and out of quickie relationships with boys her own age, but you'll be proud you influenced a small part of her life. And that you now have solid jerk-off material for the rest of time."

"Great. Still doesn't interest me."

"It should! Les, I've had several relationships with young girls, and they've all benefitted me."

"It's benefited *all* of us—in making fun of you behind your back."

"So what? Yeah, the women our age will think you're pathetic. But, the men? They'll ask for all the gory details when their wives aren't around."

Les looked over toward the young girls and start second-guessing himself.

"I couldn't."

"You *could*. Young girls are like the water cracker cleansing the palate. Of course, there are also *vintage* glasses of wine."

"Older women?"

"Awesome in their own right."

"I've never seen you give a second look to a woman who was even close to being alive in the 1970s."

"That's not true at all."

"OK?"

"I like older women. They've been there, done that, bud."

"That's good?"

"That's good and bad. Good 'cause they've done so many 'thats' they aren't phased by the kinky tendencies you've developed after getting jaded from standard missionary. An older woman would never imagine being coy about intercourse. She'll fuck you on the first date. She'll fuck you *before* the first date."

I nodded toward the corner.

"Look at those 'girls-weekend' cougars over there drinking fucking cosmos. Either of them will fuck you *tonight*. No qualms about it. You don't need to even have a first date with her. You don't need to have *any* dates with her. Older women aren't in the game to bilk a few free meals out of us."

"Don't I know about that."

"An older woman has her own job and makes her own money—much more than even you—and would rather go to nice dinners with her gal pals than with *us*. Of course, her gal pals are all married with kids, and when she tells stories about them they sound way boring. Then again, she'll call you 'That Guy' to her friends, never using your real name. "'That Guy' I've been sleeping with."

"When you see pics of her friends on Facebook, they'll look way old, which will make you remember you're fucking someone way old too. You'll have to develop constant beer goggles that mask her aging body parts. The crows feet around her eyes, the sagging neck line, aging hands. Her droopy tits, the nipples pointing perpendicular to the beautiful hardwood in her pricy doorman building. Her stomach, not fat, just doughy, fun to knead. Her ass far less so, pockmarked with cellulite, rendering sex from behind much less appealing. She'll always make you fuck with the lights off and sometimes even keep some of her clothing on too."

"Gross."

"It's not. She'll come easily, fully aware of her body. But, your favorite part about sleeping with her will be sleeping *where* she sleeps. A pricy Sleep Number bed that will be luxury personified.

"Her Sleep Number is eighteen.

"Her sexual partner number she lost count of around seventy-five.

"Her age has been thirty-nine for several years.

"You'll spend most nights 'out' with her at dark wine bars where you'll silently seethe about slugging $15-a-glass malbec. You'll go broke well before you get drunk."

"God."

"Sometimes she'll go on thousand-dollar shopping sprees. She might even buy you a nice shirt, which will instantly become the best shirt you own. You'll be worried she's trying to mold you into something you're not, but when she talks wistfully of marriage, when she laments she absolutely *has* to have a baby in the next year or two, you'll be able to tell she's not implying *with* you. She's just using you as a way station, someone to fuck because she's fucking bored."

"And that's fun?"

"The last older woman I dated, Les, we had the most pleasant break-up ever. We remained friends and I even attended her wedding! She was showing a bit on the altar." I chuckled and elbowed Les. "I even slept with one of her bridesmaids! She'd just become a divorcee and spent some of the alimony on the best fake tits I've ever touched!"

"That's great, Devin, but I don't want any of that. I just want someone like me."

"Didn't Jenn just show you, women *our* age are a huge risk!"

"How?"

"Because you have to be 100% serious with a woman your own age. We aren't getting any younger, and neither are they. But our biology doesn't matter. Theirs does. We don't need to get married this minute. They do. We don't need to have kids this second. They have to. We don't have to worry about stability, about having a nice nest egg, building college funds, posting a ton of baby pics to Facebook. They *will*. Were you completely serious with Jenn?"

"I thought so."

"You thought so?"

"I guess not. I guess all those serious conversations Jenn and I had about marriage and family…were just fiction. An imaginary future I was writing but couldn't hit 'send' on."

"Exactly! Dating a younger woman may be all shits and giggles, and an older woman just for laughs, but if you're dating someone your age, *our* current age, you are showing a serious commitment to a future with her. And you clearly weren't ready for that with Jenn. But are you ready for that with someone else, bud?"

"I'm…not sure."

"That's fine. Perhaps you only want the facile parts of a relationship."

Les was struggling to respond. Tonight he was on an emotional rollercoaster and I was locked into the seat beside him.

"Just because…it didn't turn out the way I wanted…doesn't mean that's not the way…I still want it to."

Les began fumbling with the cocktail menu, which featured full-color photographs of "unique house libation creations" such as the Mango Madness and Passionfruitopia. I sure hoped he wasn't about to start crying.

"I don't want to be single. I *can't* be single right now, Devin."

Les put his hands to his eyes, rubbing them.

"There needs to be…some sort of…relationship insurance…"

lesson number three

THE DICK AND PUSSY INSURERS

Wiping tears from your eyes, you walk toward the faceless building with the orange (pantone 144) D&PI logo on it.

The logo could be for a realtor or an ad agency. It's just your typical sleek corporate logo (Copperplate Gothic font) some founder paid a Fashion Institute of Technology student $150 to design over a weekend.

You walk through the chic lobby that could house a plastic surgeon or marketing company. Yet here men and women sit quietly crying, making this seem more like a doctor's office or upscale veterinarian. Loved ones going under the knife, cherished pets being put down.

You sit on a sofa amongst these men in Brooks Brothers suits, these women in Kate Spade skirts exuding a similar... *emotionality*. All in shock, but not quite bawling, and certainly not reading any of the magazines fanned out on the coffee table. *Cosmo*, *CityGirl*, the like. Magazines with lame dating tips written by "experts" you doubt even have sex themselves.

Your name is called, mispronounced, and mis-genderized ("Miss Ma-*han*? Miss Lesley Ma-*han*?"), and you're let in to see your agent. Heck, you haven't seen Bob since the day he sold you your policy.

It occurred just down the street, at Ink 48's swank rooftop bar. You sat sipping a Sazerac, staring at the 180-degree view of the Midtown skyline, waiting patiently for your second career date with Jenn. Bob, of course, sat sipping a Laphroig 18, neat, so hot at 96 proof it seemed fumes were coming off it. You felt if you got too close to his glass you might have to take an oxygen supply with you.

You'd ordered a Sazerac because you thought it sounded manly. And, based on its description in the leather-bound cocktail menu, you thought it would be sweet. It wasn't. Why are you always trying to turn something silly into "your" drink, Les?

"You know what else you could get for $19?" Bob asked. Bob's the rare guy who can drink alone without being creepy.

"What's that?"

"When you first sat down, you told the bartender you're about to go on your second date with this Jennifer gal…?"

"Yeah."

"Goin' well?"

"Date one went well."

"How many dates do you think this relationship will last?"

You laughed at Bob's audacious question.

"Hard to say."

"At a minimum?"

"Things could end tonight. You know some women can be fickle."

"Oh, don't I?"

"I like Jenn. She's kind. I think this relationship has serious legs."

"Tina Turner has serious legs. But what you're saying is, just two dates in, you'd be torn up if things ended?"

You found yourself answering in a most unexpected way.

"Yes. Yes I would."

"I can tell." Bob looked you up and down. "And that's why you need me, Les."

"And what do you do?"

Bob put his scotch down and rotated his barstool toward you, your knees nearly touching.

"Let me offer an analogy instead. If your house gets robbed, you got renter's insurance, right? Immediately reimburses you."

You nodded.

"Some jackass texting rear-ends you, you got car insurance?"

Again you nodded as Bob began to get real fired up.

"You get fired, Les, and unemployment *pays* you to sit on your ass drinking all day while pretending to job hunt online, correctamundo?"

"I suppose."

"They have safeguards for every other facet of life, except the *most* important…" Bob put his arm around you. "Why not dick and pussy insurance?!"

You laughed uneasily, figuring Bob was joking. That he was some business traveler who spent nights alone at hotel bars, fucking with strangers he'd never see again.

"There's no insurance for a relationship, is there? Totally out of the blue, like a robbery, a car crash, or getting laid off, you're dumped. *Andwhatareya* left with? Nothing. No companion, no one to take you to dinner, to drinks, to accompany you to the…opera."

"I don't go to the opera."

Bob looked you in the eyes, completely earnest.

"No one to *fuck you*."

Just then Jenn arrived. You were relieved, but as Jenn hugged you, Bob smoothly slipped a business card into your hands.

And that's how, back in the present, you found yourself sitting at a desk across from Robert Peters, closely examining his computer monitor.

"…and Les, it says you dated Ms. Freeman from June 8, 2012 until just a few hours ago, May 31, 2014, when she laid you off?"

"That sounds right, but I could check my Gmail archives to be 100% sure."

"No need to dredge up memories. We have the data here. Facebook ain't the only company invading your privacy. I remember when we first met. June 14th wasn't it?"

"Yes."

"I liked you from the get-go, Mr. Mann. You took out a policy with us the very next day."

Because you had awoken feeling ebullient. You and Jenn hadn't slept together but you had walked the city until the wee hours, even kissing under the moon. Trite, sure, but when romantic triteness happens to you, you don't complain.

You were in love and now wanted to spend every second with Jenn! The seconds you weren't spending with her you wanted to spend recollecting the seconds you had previously spent with her. But this incredible excitement was being tempered by an incredible fear: did she feel the same way?

On June 7 you had been single and happy. Now you were in love and scared to fucking death. The next morning, as you pulled your MetroCard from your wallet, you found it:

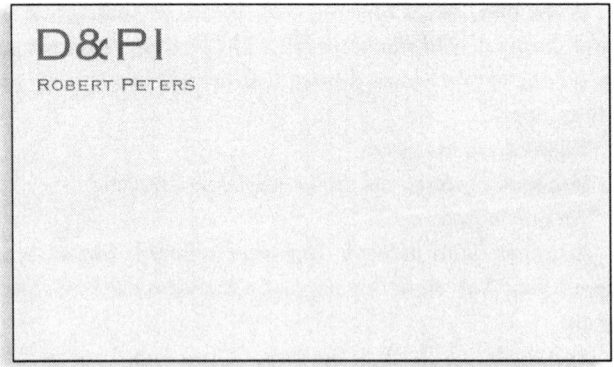

Business cards could be bought cheaply online nowadays, 1000 for $20. With so many "entrepreneurs" out there who constantly needed new business cards for new business "ventures," there was a huge industry of web companies that could make stuff for people who cared more about the facade of a business than the actual business itself.

You didn't know whether Bob had done such a thing, but you told yourself you were just curious enough to find out. That day, at lunch, you meandered back toward the west side to see if there actually were offices where Bob's card said there were. There were, and by the time your lunch hour was up, you had a D&PI plan: $18.99 a month, immediately renewed every 1st of the month on your debit card, just like that rarely-used Netflix subscription.

"And confirming, Mr. Mann, this was not a mutual split?"

"No, I was dumped."

"Did you do anything to intentionally subvert this relationship?"

"Subvert…?"

"Y'know…act like an asshole? Become passive aggressive? Cheat?"

"Absolutely not. I tried my best I swear."

"And, you're sure it's over?"

"I wish it wasn't, but I could see it in her eyes."

"Hmmmm…" Bob punches something up on his computer. "I'd like to help you, but it'll be hard to fudge this data. If you'd made it two full years you would have been in for a nice pay out, but ten days short? I just don't know."

"I'm a big boy…"

"Your premiums are going to be steep. You didn't get full coverage, only bedroom and nights."

"I set this up two years ago!"

"*Nearly.*"

"How was I to know?"

"You could have altered it at any time, Les. Probably shoulda gotten daytime and weekends too."

"I'm busy during the day, I thought I could handle it."

"You'll have to."

"Break it to me: will my company be picking up the bulk of this?"

"Mostly. Companies like yours, thankfully, want happy

employees. The broken-hearted are often unproductive."

"I was most productive when I was single. A single man has such determination to succeed. Just so stupid women will be impressed with him."

Bob nods as he continued typing.

"Unfortunately, it says Ms. Freeman had a nose job and fake breasts. We will not provide insurance pussy that has implants. That's a purely elective choice when picking a romantic partner."

You nod your head sadly.

"Also, it says Ms. Freeman did not partake in fellatio. Oral sex."

True again.

"That just breaks me up. To see a young buck like you not getting any head! How can you *get* ahead when you ain't *getting* head?!"

"I don't know…"

"The fact of the matter is, we will not provide insurance pussy that does anything Ms. Freeman didn't."

"I guess I can't miss something I never got in the first place."

"Right-o! The point of insurance pussy is to simply fill voids immediately created by a break-up. Until you can fill them yourself."

"I'm gonna next date a woman who does things with me, for me, and *to* me that I don't even want, just to say I did, and could!"

"Excellent! OK, looks like we can give you insurance pussy that is…90% as attractive, interesting, and sexually voracious as your ex."

"I didn't expect that good quite frankly."

"Well, we are the best in the biz." Bob hits a small buzzer on the underside of his desk. "You ready to meet your insurance pussy?"

You stand, nervous like you're about to go on a blind date. From a side door enters an attractive woman, indeed 90% as good-looking as Jenn.

"Hi Les! My name is…well, whatever you want it to be."

You look at Bob. "Some clients prefer to name their insurance pussy after their recently lost ex, while others like to go with something completely new."

You think about it for a second.

"How 'bout Stacy? I've always had a notion I'd like to date a Stacy."

"Stacy it is."

Stacy leans in to hug you. Your screwy mind wonders what Stacy's deal is. Does she get paid for this gig? Does she have to give up her life for yours? And, what does she do in her spare time? Does she date anyone? Does she consider herself a prostitute? Should you consider yourself a john?

Unfortunately, according to the thick non-disclosure contract you signed, you're not allowed to ask her any of these inane questions, nor can she legally answer them. You feel like someone trying to figure out the science behind a time travel movie. Probably best to just accept an unrealistic premise and pretend it's your new reality.

"Let's go get a drink, Les. I've read your bio, but I think we have some catching up to do."

You're instantly charmed by Stacy, this phony stand-in girlfriend. You feel better about your life already. Being alone that first night, or with the boys, eating buffalo wings, getting drunk on cheap beer, going on a fucking mindless bar crawl and hitting on drunk skanks with me...then heading home alone to masturbate, that would feel pathetic. Just *pathetic*. But not this. Not this! Not this insurance pussy. Nope. Not pathetic at all.

"Always glad to get a fella back on his feet, Mr. Mann," Bob says. "But, remember...you only get her for the next seventy-five days. We expect you to be healed by then."

📍 **Sven** (Columbus Circle) | 10:30 PM

chapter six

WHY COULD YOU SAY OF NEW YORK: "BRIGHT LIGHTS, BIG TITTIES"?

"Why do I tell you about my dates if you're just going to use them to make fun of me down the road?"

Les remained silent until an Aryan's wet dream of a bartender—tall, muscular, towheaded, efficient—came over to take our drink orders.

"Gimme a Sazerac," Les snapped.

I laughed. "Yeah, make it two."

The bartender went off to consult his iPad mixology app and I turned back toward Les.

"Seriously, though, 'insurance pussy'?"

"I actually think it sounds pretty great."

"Yes. In fact, it's such a great idea, I'm almost surprised it doesn't already exist."

I pulled up Safari on my iPhone and Les instantly bent back my pointer finger.

"What the fuck?!"

"Don't!"

"Why?"

"Don't you know there are people who monitor all Google searches?"

"So?"

"If they see something interesting they immediately copyright it, buy up domains, trademarks. Everything."

"That's not how it works."

I took a step back and gave Les the Heisman pose to make some space. After a few seconds, I showed him my screen:

> Your search - **dick & pussy insurers** - did not match any documents.
>
> Suggestions:
>
> - Make sure all words are spelled correctly.
> - Try different keywords.
> - Try more general keywords.

"Take out the ampersand?"

"It's a stupid idea, Les. Even in a city full of dumb startups, Dick and Pussy Insurers is a terrible fucking idea."

"Yeah, you should know about dumb startups."

Dejected, Les finally took a sip of his Sazerac. He winced. "So…?"

"Tastes like…whiskey mixed with black licorice."

Les slumped down in his seat. I could tell he was sad, not just because he had lost Jennifer Freeman as his girlfriend, but because he had lost everything that came with that: companionship, plans, hugs and kisses, sex.

And he was now stuck with me. We watched a group of men enter who were either American homosexuals or European tourists. They took selfies with each other. Les perked up again.

"Oooh, OK, then how 'bout this idea? What if you could hire someone to pose with you in pics you could upload to social media? You know, like me and a really hot girl."

"Why would you want to do that?"

"It might make Jenn jealous."

"So you'd approach a pretty girl and ask for a photo with her as opposed to asking her for a…date, a kiss, a handjob in the bathroom?!"

"Well…"

"Talk about asocial media."

"Then what?!" Les whined.

"See girls for who they really are! That's the only real pussy insurance in this world."

A bachelorette party entered the bar, wearing stupid props. Tiaras, boas, glittery t-shirts with sayings on them ("Buy the Bride a Beer"). Women always became Carrot Top the second their friend became a bachelorette.

"I see…skanks who looked like they robbed a Spencer's Gifts."

"Don't judge books by their covers."

"If those women were books, their dust jackets would already be on some douche's bedroom floor. It's time I leave New York. I'm sick of the women here. My options might be better in another city."

"Options for what? You think you're going to meet high-quality women in Tulsa or Des Moines?"

"Maybe."

"Les, a 10 out of 10 in Tulsa is like a 3 here."

"Bullshit."

"This is the greatest city in the world to meet women."

"Yeah, if you like a certain type. But, they're all the same type. New York women are New York women. And I'm tired of them."

"That's not true at all. Each neighborhood in each borough has a different kind of New York woman."

DEVIN'S TRAVEL GUIDE
to stereotyping NYC women

MIDTOWN
Looks like: bright lights, big titties!
Lives in: doormanned high-rise.
Works at: Condé Nast niche magazine where her business card says "editor," though her e-mails make it seem she can hardly spell.
In bed: uses tips learned from *Cosmo*, struggles to make you come, but damn if she doesn't keep going for it.

UPPER EAST SIDE
Looks like: iPhone (still on her parents' plan) glued to her ear, wearing Lululemon yoga pants and carrying a mat, even though she hasn't been to class any time recently. Yoga mats are motorcycle helmets for women.
Lives in: high-rise daddy pays for, close to noisy Second Avenue subway construction.
Works at: financial institution.
In bed: shows her youth. Was fucking drunken fratboys just 250 days ago so will frequently intone how you are "good in bed," even though you don't do anything special.

UPPER WEST SIDE
Looks like: a MILF, even though she's not a mom yet, though you do LF her.
Lives in: pre-war complex that you, at first, assume is a nursing home.

Works at: private high school where yearly tuition is more than her yearly salary.
In bed: so inhibited she constantly analyzes the coitus while in media coitus. Makes you get a full STD test before you have vaginal sex for the first time.

CHELSEA
Looks like: doughy body gone doughier from trite cupcake obsession.
Lives in: rent-controlled studio, well-decorated with legitimate artwork. And cats.
Works at: museum you didn't even know existed (MoHair) as a curator of exhibits you can't believe anyone would possibly pay to see.
In bed: gives incredible head, likes being dominated, when drunk insinuates her friend Bobby could join in if you were interested in a devil's threesome.

MURRAY HILL
Looks like: curly-headed JAP.
Lives in: dorm-like high-rise, a messy 4 BR with the bathroom covered in hair care products.
Works at: low on the totem pole in publishing, considering an MBA if she could ever skip happy hour just once to study her Princeton Review books.
In bed: only gives blowjobs until she can get away with not, and sleeps in shorts with her sorority letters (ΔΔΔ) on the ass.

EAST VILLAGE
Looks like: skinny with tats and piercings in places she thinks interesting but you find repulsive.
Lives in: piece of shit loft in Alphabet City.

Works at: bartender at a place only unemployed dickheads hang out at.

In bed: you can't remember. You always wake up next to her after pounding PBR and Jack shots ($5 special) all night at a dive with an old-fashioned jukebox full of Lou Reed and New York Dolls. You slip out, shocked how few people are up in the East Village during morning rush hour.

WEST VILLAGE

Looks like: wears clothes you know are expensive even though they are from some "boutique" you've never heard of.

Lives in: gorgeous brownstone her aunt uses as a pied-à-terre when back in America (which is never, though damn if you're not curious where she sleeps when this does ultimately occur).

Works at: nowhere. Occasionally curates art for a friend's gallery.

In bed: standard missionary.

SOHO

Looks like: "Hey, haven't I seen you on an H&M billboard in Times Square?!"

Lives in: full-time resident of a swank hotel you didn't realize was a hotel.

Works at: model.

In bed: too coked up to care, body so flexible you're borderline grossed out as you learn more about anatomy than you did in AP biology.

TRIBECA

Looks like: young and nubile, smokes Parliaments

like a little kid licking a Tootsie Pop.
Lives in: massive condo with twenty-five foot ceilings.
Works at: intern for someone famous.
In bed: you only make out on street corners after she insists on buying you dinner and drinks at a hotel bar because she "forgot" her driver's license and couldn't get into the place you'd originally chosen. She never invites you back to her place and never sleeps over at yours. Make sure she is not still in high school.

FINANCIAL DISTRICT
Looks like: uptight and proper, doesn't own a pair of blue jeans and has never let her hair down. Is so unaware of pop culture you think she's fucking with you ("No seriously, who is Kanye?").
Lives in: doorman building on a street you didn't even know people lived on.
Works at: investment bank across the street from said building.
In bed: rarely, due to ninety-hour work weeks. When she is she's sleeping like a coma patient...until her Blackberry explodes from an early morning e-mail from her manager.

HARLEM
Looks like: mixed race, but you will count it as finally banging a black chick.
Lives in: brownstone.
Works at: poet at a coffee shop she is also a barista at.
In bed: passionate. Which doesn't translate to..."fuckable."

BROOKLYN
Looks like: Women's Studies major.
Lives in: neighborhood you didn't realize was gentrified, has a backyard complete with a hammock and overturned milk crates to sit on and smoke weed.
Works at: sometimes deals a little weed, sometimes stagehands at an experimental theater company, writes lots of comments on Gawker and Jezebel.
In bed: less experimental, and surprisingly conservative. Enjoys doing drugs and just laying on her air mattress staring at the ceiling.

QUEENS
Looks like: grade-A skank of ambiguous ethnicity, with dark hair almost flowing into sideburns.
Lives in: row house with mom and dad and a nativity scene in the tiny yard out front, even though Christmas is nowhere close.
Works at: waitress at father's restaurant, attending community college at night (45 credits shy of her Associate's).
In bed: very quiet as she doesn't want her parents to hear. When finished, you're forced to jump out her window like a middle schooler.

STATEN ISLAND
Looks like: someone from a high school yearbook. From 1989.
Lives in: you have no interest in finding out.
Works at: Wall Street law firm paralegal.
In bed: you've always wanted to fuck on a boat. Now you will. The Staten Island Ferry.

"You're such a bigot."

"Why?"

"Everything you said was pure stereotyping."

"New York women want to be seen as stereotypes!"

As we crossed 57th Street, we looked west down it, toward the Hudson.

"Well…what about Jersey?"

"Pass."

"The Bronx?"

"I'm not sure. I've never been besides Yankee games."

"Typical. So why this neighborhood tonight?"

"Because Les, there's no better spot than Hell's Kitchen on a Friday night. Everyone has just come from work and you can encounter a large variety before each goes home to its niche."

"Bitches with niches and I have seen plenty of the *large* variety."

"I'm certain you'll find someone at this next spot."

"Wher—"

Just then, Les saw the iconic fat pig in the distance.

"Come on—Rudy's?!"

"There's always chatty women there."

"Chatties or fatties?"

We entered the filthy dive.

"I have a plan for you and, just like a born again Christian, you should relinquish your powers to me."

"God help me."

I inhaled the delightful fumes of stale beer, snow-shoed through the sawdust-covered floors, and backhanded shelled peanuts off the decrepit bar so we could lean on it.

"Rudy's makes Drunx look like the 21 Club."

"Hey, that's about the age of the girls currently here. Perfect!"

I ordered the house beer, Rudy's Red. The surly bartender quickly gave us back a pitcher only half full, a Miracle Whip-like head of amber foam topping it off. As I struggled to pour us each a full plastic cup of actual beer, Les noticed that some jokers had added bar garbage to his knick-knacks box.

"Jesus!"

He removed a few crumpled cocktail napkins, tiny swizzle sticks, and maraschino cherry stems, tossing them onto the floor.

"Could you leave that stupid thing in an alley? Because it's that box that's cockblocking you. Cock*box*ing you. Box blocking your cock from…boxes…"

"Quite the wordsmith." Les sarcastically cheers'd me with his beer.

We had both just put our cups to our mouths when we heard her voice.

"You just get laid off?"

📍 **Rudy's** (w. 44ᵗʰ St. and Ninth Ave.)

chapter seven
WHAT EVER HAPPENED TO JOB SECURITY?

"You just get laid off?"

The question hung in the air.

While beer foam hung on Les's upper lip like a milk mustache.

"Huh…?"

Two attractive women stood behind us. The ones we'd spied at Drunx just a few hours earlier. Their slightly glazed eyes and crooked smiles told me they'd enjoyed a few cocktails in the intervening hours.

"Well it looks like you just got laid off from…"

The brunette rifled through Les's box: a Nerf basketball hoop, a tennis racket, some novelty boxer shorts ("The Fuck Starts Here"), *The Godfather* DVD box set (Part III still in the cellophane), a bottle of Johnnie Walker Gold, and an opened twelve-pack of Durex condoms (eleven remaining).

"…the best job in the world?!"

She smiled at Les, but he, of course, had no idea how to respond.

"Let's see…drink the scotch, then drop the shorts, then put

on the condom, then…SWISH!"

She laughed heartily. It would have been cruel if it wasn't so funny.

"But that doesn't explain the…tennis racket? Hmmm…any ideas, Erin?"

Erin shrugged.

"Come on, leave him alone, Cheryl."

Sensing Les's distress, I had no choice but to save him. I turned my iPhone spotlight onto both women.

Erin pushed my phone down as she and Cheryl slid between us to order drinks. They looked of an indeterminate age in that way where it's always hard to tell the age of attractive women in their twenties or thirties. Attractive women in their thirties always looked to be in their twenties and the reverse was true for those in their twenties.

Les finally, and loudly, answered the question that had already floated away.

"Uh, no, I haven't been laid off. I…uh…I just got…dumped by my girlfriend today. Actually."

Erin turned back toward Les, studying him curiously. Cheryl impatiently tapped her black flat as the bartender tended to the free hotdogs rolling on a cooker behind the bar. I tried to flirtatiously lock eyes with her. Silences scared Les, so he spoke up again just to speak.

"But, *fuck* her, huh?!"

Erin smiled, but in a way like she was almost surprised by her natural reaction.

"Yeah, well, I just dumped my boyfriend too. So, *fuck* him, huh?!"

She turned back toward the bar, squinting her gaze at the bar's plastic-bottled vodka selection, looking for something in particular. She wasn't going to find it here. I didn't recognize a single brand, many written in languages I couldn't even identify: Takaa, Vision, Brother Nikolav. Meanwhile, Cheryl finally caught my gaze and returned it with a smile, now refusing to break eye contact, as if this was a staring contest with money on the line.

"But you're right…"

Erin turned back to Les. "Huh?" She seemed to have an underlying sadness.

"About getting laid off. Getting dumped *is* like getting laid off."

It was I who lost the staring contest, breaking eyes to regard Les with a "What are you fucking doing?!" glare.

"How so?" Erin seemed dubious.

"I mean…look at our parents." Les was speaking nervously, a little too fast, a little too wavering. "They took jobs right out of college and kept them for life. That was something to be proud of. Starting with a tiny desk in the middle of the floor, moving to a cubicle around the exterior, then a small office, then a larger office, then a corner office, then the boss's office where you started counting down the days 'til you could retire with that engraved Timex."

"Why does a retired person need to know the time any how?" She was trying to make a joke.

"Uh…but nowadays, there's no job security. Look at people's LinkedIn profiles."

"Isn't that just Facebook without bikini pics?" Cheryl snarked.

"Uh…I mean. Yeah. My point is, most people have had a dozen jobs before they're thirty. And when you meet a person that's had one job for, *Jesus*, like five straight years, you wonder…"

"'What is wrong with you?'"

I was thinking the exact same thing. About Les, though.

"Right! So we keep our résumés polished, make sure our interview skills are sharp, always dress for success. We never know when we're going to need an exit strategy, or when we're going to be forced into one."

Erin smiled, nodding in what seemed like some sort of agreement.

"It's the same with dating. We don't stay with someone for

life. Are you kidding me? We look at the people who have had one partner their whole life, and think, 'What a total loser.'"

I returned my gaze toward Cheryl, rolling my eyes at Les and Erin's conversation. Cheryl nodded back conspiratorially. She carried a beat-up paperback in her hand, tucked to her chest like a running back holding a football, its cover turned inward. I playfully angled my head to try and see the title. She noticed, and at first assumed I was checking out her breasts, which bared just a hint of shadowy cleavage at the top of her purple sweater. They were why the word "ample" had been invented and I wanted a sample. After realizing I actually just wanted to see the book's title, she spun it around, holding it up proudly. I nodded, impressed.

"That's why our parents don't quite understand us. They don't understand a world so lacking in loyalty, always looking for a better opportunity. But, what are the chances your best job opportunity came along in your early twenties? That you met that girl for a lifetime in college?"

"Minimal?"

"*Overwhelmingly* minimal odds. Our parents played it safe because, back then, taking the first thing that came along was safe. Trying to find something better was risky. But now, the risk is in being safe!"

Whereas Les would not shut up once he got a woman in his sights, I was now at the point where I could pick up a woman without even talking to her. I'd hooked up with a deaf girl the previous summer, had snagged countless foreign tourists at shitty bars like Gastro!, and I'd even picked up a girl *while* she was acting in an off-Broadway musical about Betsy Ross. Les and Jenn had dragged me along to that boring shit.

Erin stared at Les, not sure how to respond to his weird, little rant.

"Metaphorically, of course, right? You should *always* wear a condom."

She took the Durex box out and playfully dumped condoms all over Les's lap, smiling, as he fumbled to catch them all.

I could see Les immediately falling for her, her beautiful, big smile, sassy attitude, bossiness. That nerd Les was surely thinking: "I'd like to add you to my professional network."

Cheryl was finally able to grab her drink order—a PBR can, and a yellowish cocktail that she handed to Erin—as she turned back toward Les.

"You poor guy…"

"Les. I'm Les."

"Well you might have heard that I'm Cheryl. And that lady you've been charming the pants on is Erin."

"Nice to meet you…Erin."

"You need to cheer up, Les. You really do. Things will be all right if you just remember one thing..."

Cheryl grabbed Les by his collar and shook him vigorously, rattling his pickled brain and kickstarting his hangover before it had even begun.

"You can act like a man!!! What's the matter with you? Is this how you turned out? A Hollywood *finocchio* that cries like a woman?"

Cheryl playfully slapped Les's cheek and slowly stuffed a free bar hotdog into his face. I had no clue what had just transpired. Cheryl turned back to me and, noticing my confusion, spoke to me for the first time since entering Rudy's.

"It's from *The Godfather*. When Don Corleone lays into Johnny Fontane."

She pulled the DVD set from Les's box and handed it to me.

"Oh. I've never seen it."

"You've never seen *The Godfather*?!"

"Everyone talks about it so much, I figured, I know what happens, what's the point?"

Cheryl looked at me, shaking her head with a smile. "You're incredible."

Erin warmly touched Les's face where Cheryl had slapped it, whispering to him as he chewed his hot dog.

"If you ask me, breaking up is less like getting laid off…and more like dying. Some days I feel like a ghost, wandering this city aimlessly, unable to communicate with all the people I used to communicate with, only able to spy on them from above."

"Or, on Facebook!" Les added.

Erin suddenly looked embarrassed. Cheryl leaned in to now save her.

"No one can enjoy the present for the future. Did you know the average couple gets engaged two years, eight months, and seven days after their first date?"

"Where'd you read that?" I butted in, trying to quickly do some math in my head.

"*Read*? I saw it on New York One."

Cheryl pointed up to the bar's tube television, muted 11:00 PM NY1 news, another story about how fat kids today were. It now took the average adult two hands to lift the Happy Meal box. They were going to have to add luggage wheels to it soon.

Erin looked shocked as she turned to Cheryl. "So Joe and I were at the engagement precipice and I let him go?!"

"And Jenn and I were just seven months and twenty-two days from that average engagement number. I hear ya. Now I gotta start all over again at day zero with someone else."

Les met eyes with Erin just a split second before turning away, their faces flushed from embarrassment, or maybe just from the glowing red Schlitz sign reflecting off them.

"Maybe Jenn was never meant for you in the first place," I noted.

"What do you mean?"

"Maybe she was *not* interested in you as a person, but only in the end-goal of marriage. Any guy woulda worked. Any dude woulda done. Any dick woulda—"

"All right!"

I stood up and got in their faces. Erin looked scared and took a step back. Meanwhile, poor Les nearly fell off his stool, having to grab Erin's waist to steady himself.

"Just because you took the wrong fork in the road, doesn't mean you shouldn't turn back. There's no such thing as sunk costs in the relationship game." I sat back down, thinking.

"Except for a kid, of course."

Cheryl laughed hard, before looking at Erin.

"I think what Devin's trying to say is: maybe your exes *weren't* failures. Maybe, they were successes."

"Yeah. That's it."

lesson number four

THERE IS NO SUCH THING AS "THE ONE(S) WHO GOT AWAY"

Now, this chain hotel wasn't as nice as those named to evoke serene nature. You know, the Four Seasons or DoubleTree. Nor was it as bad as those that flat-out tell you about their quality in the name. Comfort Inn isn't comfortable, Holiday Inn is no holiday and, of course, Quality Inn is just shit.

I sat at the worst table in the Sheraton's reception hall. The worst table at a wedding is like the final chair in the high school band. One more slip-up and you won't be attending any more performances. I'd already attended far too many weddings in my life.

At my table sat four boring couples I barely acknowledged. In fact, the floral eclipse of a centerpiece was so large it blocked their faces. Perfect. It made my lack of conversation less awkward during the time I was less drunkard.

I, on the other hand, was coupled with a tween. "Elijah" according to his placecard.

"Who you related to?"

"Cousin of the bride. They had no room for me at a real table so I'm back here with you assholes."

I was clearly the last asshole invited to the event and, thus, was forced to stay at the crummy motel across the highway. Based on the come-speckled comforter, it appeared few people used the Sleep Inn correctly either. I gave Elijah my gin and tonic and ordered two more.

"This vodka tastes like…pine cones."

Elijah winced.

"That's the juniper, bud."

"Jupiter?"

The kid was already deeply confused, and I didn't feel like giving him a lesson on botany. His brain was already getting one on chemistry. He'd be having one on biology by the end of the night, throwing up everywhere. Best if I was already back at the Fuck Inn by then getting my own lesson on anatomy from a wedding guest.

"Help me out, kid. Look around for any hot girls."

I wasn't sure why I kept going to weddings. They never got any more exciting. Perhaps that's why people actually got married—just to wager an attempt at having a better wedding than their friends'. But it was always the same for a guest:

Hit the church where you immediately check how big the program is. One page folded over and printed at Kinko's, great. Several pages, *stapled* with a spine, you were going to be there awhile. The more "Jesus" you saw, the worse.

Of course, cocktail hour is the best part of any wedding. In fact, I've always thought they should open a restaurant called Cocktail Hour:

Cocktail Hour, *bring to the real world the awesome experience of standing around schmoozing while a never-ending stream of finger foods emerge from the kitchen, all while getting shit-canned at an open bar packed with horny babes in party dresses.*

If cocktail hours were fun, then wedding dinners were boring as fuck. Just like this one. We'd already watched the wedding party enter and try to be funny with some awkward dancing, surely praying the video would go viral and get them a *Today* show invite. Now we were listening to the best man and maid of honor talk everyone to sleep. The audience was becoming restless, hungry, dipsomaniacal, wanting to dance, wanting to potentially fuck someone, wanting to be free.

"The fact of the matter is, Elijah, the only difference between the quality of weddings is the *quantity* of single women available. You see anyone yet?"

"No."

"Yeah, well, getting any girl back to the Fuck Inn is going to be pretty tough as is."

"Whoa, check out *her*!" Elijah nodded across the room.

"Ugh."

"She's pretty hot, huh?"

"Unfortunately not."

"*Unfortunately*?!"

"That's Kaylee."

"Who?"

"I used to date her."

"You used to date *her*?!"

"Can't believe it, right? I'm totally out of her league. *Now*. But back freshman year we were in the same league. The Yankees and Red Sox…if they fucked like nympho dorm bunnies."

I decided to now give Elijah a history lesson.

"Sometimes I wonder where my life would be if the three serious relationships in my past hadn't ended."

"Sometimes I wonder what would have happened if I hadn't dumped Britney Gordon in 6th grade."

"Have you even had your sex-ed assembly yet?!"

"First time I saw a vagina!"

I laughed.

"But what if I hadn't broken up with Kaylee at the end of junior year?"

Next to Kaylee sat some bozo who looked just like me. If I were fatter with thinner hair. If I wore Men's Warehouse suits. If I thought cufflinks with baseballs on them were acceptable in public.

"We would be living in Albany. I'd have a job I hated, a wife I hated, a dick I masturbated. I'd never get laid and the rare times

I did, it would produce kid after kid after miserable kid."

Three little kids, spaced an impossibly short amount of time apart, came running through the tables and jumped on Kaylee's husband's lap. He winced, the clear after-effects of a recent vasectomy or rec league soccer mishap.

The waiter came by with two gin and tonics, confused when I took both.

"You think he's onto us?" Elijah worried.

"Catering folks don't give a fuck. They only give a quick fuck to each other."

"In the kitchen?"

"Between *courses*. 'And did you RSVP for the strip or salmon, sir? That caterer's herpes or my chlamydia, ma'am?'"

"Well, what about her?"

Elijah nodded across the room at an impeccably dressed woman.

"Becky? Becky was the first girl I dated after college!"

Elijah was shocked I had such a history. A history that was now history.

"Back when I dated Becky she was a real party girl. We seemed to have the same pleasures, the same aspirations. In retrospect, we didn't. Becky didn't *really* want to party every night. It was just a seduction ploy. She always wanted a ring, wanted to be a rich housewife, wanted to live in Scarsdale or Darien or another boring suburb. After thirteen months dating me, it must have been clear I would never fit that bill."

Beside Becky sat her husband who also looked like me, if I could afford perfectly tailored Hugo Boss suits, Ferragamo loafers, a Patek Philippe watch, and a paunch of a belly created by an expense account's worth of dinners at various Ruth's Chrises around our fine nation.

"Becky doesn't care about her husband, she doesn't care about her kids."

"Where are they?" Elijah wondered.

"Probably back home with the Swedish au pair."

"I have a Norwegian one."

"The rich Manhattan parents take a Scandinavian au pair. The Scandinavian au pair in Brooklyn takes a Jamaican nanny. The Jamaican nanny lets her kids roam free in Queens. Hi ho the derry-oh, the latchkey kid nicknamed 'Cheese' (he never smiles) lives alone."

Becky fondled the expensive jewels around her neck while her husband slugged his scotch and histrionically winced like it was the worst rotgut he'd ever tasted.

"Shitty scotch selection here, Becks. Nothing better than… *Black Label*."

"All Becky ever wanted was a fancy-free existence of glitzy dinner parties and afternoon shopping sprees. Finding a rich sap of a man who would allow that so long as she married him and shit out kids was her conduit to facilitate such a lifestyle."

"At least it's not 'Red,'" Becky droned, like she'd heard it countless times before.

"I could have been that man. I made decent money when we were going out. But what kind of life would that be? I don't rue the fact Becky dumped me when I refused to propose with a $15,000 ring after only a year of dating." I thought for a second. "Huh, it would be our seven-year anniversary by now. What one is the seven-year? The brass ball or the steel chain?"

Elijah took a sip of his G&T and continued scanning the room.

"So you see, I could have chosen any of these other routes in life, Elijah. But, luckily, I trusted my gut."

"My gut feels woozy."

"Drink some water, here, uh…"

I grabbed the centerpiece, pulled the flowers out, and handed the kid the clear vase. He greedily chugged the light green water. The four couples began whispering about the off-centered fourteen-year-old drinking from the centerpiece, craning their necks to try and spot any adult supervision.

"Devin?"

With the centerpiece gone I now looked across the table to see…

"Miriam?"

I started laughing maniacally. The kid was wobbling in his seat. I yanked down on his lapel and he bolted upright like a living marionette.

"Now what idiot thought to seat my beloved ex across from me?"

"I'm wondering the same exact thing."

"Fuckin' wedding planner, huh?"

Miriam was my longest relationship ever. I was older and wiser by the time I dated her. Or, so I thought.

"It's nice to see you, Devin. You look…well."

"Well…*what*?"

Miriam was sweet and nice. But she was stifling. She didn't want to have fun, didn't champion my dreams, and had I stayed with her I'd no doubt be a real estate agent in Ft. Meyers by now. Selling pink fucking houses to red fucking necks.

"Congrats on your success, Devin. Ya in the market for anything?"

Miriam's husband robotically handed me his business card.

"Gotta lotta great properties openin' up! In this recession, it's a buyer's market down South!"

Miriam politely nodded, unenthusiastically. I turned toward Elijah, now wobbling like an ocean buoy, slurring his words like a stroke victim. Feeding him booze was actually a stroke of genius. And so was he.

"Wha' about her? She must be single."

Buzzed Elijah noticed a tall blonde at the table next to ours, sitting between two other women clinging onto men.

"She's pretty hot."

"No, she's *really* hot, but I am a bit of a grade inflator."

"My dick's inflating. Tell me you haven't…"

"I haven't."

Elijah smiled wide as I looked around the room. At Kaylee, Becky, and Miriam. I felt like someone who had died and come back to see what the world was like without him. That may have shook up Ebenezer Scrooge, but it just made me giddy. I would have been Ebenezer Screwed if I'd stayed with any of them.

"*Do you remember…?*"

The DJ's iPod struck up a stirring rendition of Earth, Wind, and Fire's "September."

"I just realized there's something more important than the fact I live an interesting life, Elijah. The most important thing is that I am free. Remember Pinocchio?"

"Is he in Wu Tang?"

I looked at the blonde as she shook her ass on the dance floor.

"He's not a rapper, but there is a song he sang."

I turned back toward Elijah, but he had suddenly disappeared. To where, I'll never know. I stood, and the stiff gin and tonics finally hit me. The room became animated like a Disney movie. Every step another hand-drawn cel. Of course, I've intentionally neglected to mention to you all that I'd shared a bag of shrooms with the caterers while waiting for the other guests to arrive from the church ceremony I'd accidentally skipped on purpose.

I patted Miriam on the head and began singing, hoping none of Disney's intellectual property lawyers were wedding guests:

> "*I've got no strings*
> *To hold me down*
> *To make me fret,*
> *or make me frown…*

I danced by Becky and patted her head.

> *I had strings*
> *But now I'm free*
> *There are no strings on me*"

I touched Kaylee on her shoulder. She wasn't animated, she was hardly moving. I reached the tall blonde gyrating her hips like she was at a strip club. There's just something about a woman getting married that makes all the other females in attendance so goddamn horny. Like if they fucked a tuxedoed stranger they too would wake up with a diamond on their finger and a trip to Aruba.

"Hi, I'm Devin, the groom's intramural basketball teammate," I said. Or something.

"I'm Amanda, the bride's second cousin, twice removed," she said. Or something.

"Are you single?"

"I am."

"Then would you like to come back to the Sleep Inn and hear me tell a lie?

📍 Bloopers (w. 43rd St. and Eleventh Ave.) | 11:59 PM

chapter 8

WHY DO SOME MEN THINK BEING AN ASSHOLE TO WOMEN MAKES THEM AN "ALPHA MALE"?

"That did not work!"

"I'm more surprised your lines at Rudy's *did* work."

"Shhhh…"

Cheryl and Erin had invited us to join them at Bloopers, a new sports bar that didn't show sports. Live ones at least.

"Those weren't 'lines.'"

"I know. They were an abomination."

We followed Erin and Cheryl through the packed joint, Les whispering to me so they couldn't hear him. On the bar's TVs, a grainy clip showed a 1970s-era base runner face-planting while rounding third.

"I can't help but think Jenn is the one who got away."

"If on the day you'd met Jenn you were given a glimpse of what she desired in the future, would you have ever dated her in the first place?!"

"Uh…"

"You *never* would have dated her."

"I might…"

"You wouldn't have."

"I think I would—"

"Don't get me wrong, bud, you would have slept with her a few times. But you *never* would have dated her."

Cheryl and Erin glanced back over their shoulders, smiling at us. On the TVs, Derrick Coleman airballed a foul shot.

"Listen to me: *you* were the one who got away, Les. It was you. Now go talk to Erin."

"I don't know."

"Do it."

"Hitting on women in 2014 is like being in a fucking improv comedy troupe. I'm just sick of it."

"How can you be in your thirties, and drunk, yet still have so little of a clue? Keep this going. For whatever reason she invited you to follow her here. So follow *her*!"

I dragged Les like a misbehaving schoolchild toward Erin and Cheryl and just as he was about to say something, everyone's smartphone struck midnight. The TVs went black and a silence came over the room. And all eyes looked upward.

The TVs came back on, now showing footage of a woman in the shower getting railed from behind. It was jarring. But, all of the sudden, the porn star slipped and, reaching for the shower curtain rod to try and stabilize herself, she instead pulled it down in the process. It fell on top of her and her male co-star in one giant heap. Bloopers' crowd erupted, including Erin. I would have guessed she was too prim.

Two men noticed her laughing and quickly approached.

"Shit!"

Les was instantly deflated.

"You should have acted quicker, bud."

"I had no plan."

"With women, *speed* is better than having a plan. Uh, except in bed of course."

On the TVs, a porn star getting jackhammered accidentally kicked the cameraman in the face when he moved in for a close-up.

Now Les was just frustrated. He began lashing out, no longer whispering whatsoever.

"Whoa, we are such cool New Yorkers who think it's *perfectly* normal to be in a bar showing pornography! Stupid hipsters."

"Don't take your anger out on the porn bloopers. Anyhow, those guys aren't hipsters, just creeps."

We listened in on the men now hitting on Erin and Cheryl.

"I guess I'll decide eventually if I feel comfortable telling you my name," one of the men confidently noted.

"But you came up to me," Erin noted.

"You were in my path, so I figured, 'Why not?'"

"OK, then if I don't get to know your name, what should I call you?" Erin asked with a smile.

"You can call me 'Don't-Know-My-Name.' And you can call my friend 'Don't-Know-His-Name.'"

Don't-Know-His-Name grabbed Cheryl and Erin's hands and went in to kiss them, but mere inches from doing so, he retracted.

"I just realized I don't know where these filthy things have been!"

He histrionically wiped his own hand off on the back of his jeans.

"Hey!" Erin playfully slapped him. "They're clean." She giggled.

"Does anyone here have some Purell?!" the guy shouted out, looking around.

On the TVs, a porn star choked on a come shot, forcing her co-star to give the Heimlich.

"I need a drink."

Les headed to the bar and I followed.

"Don't worry about those assholes."

"Why shouldn't I? Their shit is going to work on Erin and Cheryl."

"No it won't."

"Yeah it will."

"Why do you say that, Les?"

"Because…" he looked at me, "It's the same kind of asshole shit you say to girls. And it works for you."

Aaron Goldfarb | 89

"Whoa, wait a second. I am not an asshole."

"OK."

"I may sometimes speak the truth and that may sometimes get ugly, but I am not an asshole. Those guys…?" I looked back toward them. "Pure fucking phonies with fake asshole personas. Someone told them this shit would work for them. They probably read it on some dumbass Pick-Up Artist manosphere blog."

Like many in the Pick-Up Artist (PUA) community, I would have bet anything that Don't-Know-My-Name and Don't-Know-His-Name had surely once been big-league dorks. Like Les, the two had surely seen cocky assholes always surrounded by women, but never quite understood why. So I would have bet anything they went to countless seminars to try and figure these things out. They had surely once ordered massive DVD sets, purchased audiobooks, and even hired personal dating coaches to tag along with them, all of which, and whom, had taught them how to become: "Alpha Males."

These Alpha Males had surely scripted personas for themselves and created canned lines and flow charts for all flirting situations. They'd surely used the lines they had just used on Cheryl and Erin hundreds of times before.

On the TVs, a porn star accidentally farted in the face of the man eating her out. He retched for a second before throwing up.

"So, if we don't get your names…can we ask what you guys *do*?" Erin wondered.

"You can ask."

"Doesn't mean we'll tell."

"Then I'll ask: 'What do you guys do?'"

"Don't-Know-His-Name and I just got back from spelunking in Indonesia. Do you dummies know what that is?"

"Naw, she probably doesn't know what that is. She looks like she went to community college."

Erin cut them off. "I know what it is. I played *Carmen Sandiego* when I was a kid."

"So, like, up 'til just a year or two ago?" Don't-Know-My-

Name joked.

I nodded toward Les.

"Just watch them. Watch how stilted and constructed their replies are. Pretty standard asshole game moves. Insults. 'Negs,' they used to call them. Making fun of the girl to make her feel inferior to them."

"Why?"

"I guess the theory being that inferior females would want to have sex with any male they thought superior to them, in order to, you know, like boost their own inferiority to some level of superiority."

"That's stupid. That doesn't work."

"It does sometimes…"

It seemed to be this time too.

"You're right. It does…"

After grabbing some more beer, we continued watching the men seemingly winning over Cheryl and Erin.

"Simply by being assholes!" Les exclaimed to me, now enchanted by their behavior.

On the TVs, two porn stars fucking on a shoreline were interrupted when a massive wave came in, washing over their doggy-style sex and taking the female out to sea where she choked on the water, proving she did indeed have a gag reflex for salty fluids.

"Put your number right here for me. Assuming you're literate."

Erin smiled some more and we watched as she scribbled her phone number down for Don't-Know-His-Name. He and his buddy proudly marched past us and toward the bar. Les looked at them, then me.

"My fucking nightmare. I can't believe this shit! I've talked like a fucking nice guy chump to Erin for over an hour—and it took those assholes just seconds!"

Les impetuously followed them to the bar.

"Maybe I should start being more of an asshole to women, you think?"

He called out to them.

"Seriously?! You dorks are impressed you got a number?! How 'bout them apples, right?"

The two men stopped dead in their tracks and turned around.

On the TVs, a porn star got a dildo stuck in her vagina, forcing the boom mic man and several other crew members to fish around inside of her, like a rescue team trying to save a child fallen down a country well.

"Oh look, it's Will Cunting." Don't-Know-My-Name smiled cockily. "Jealous?"

"Why would I be jealous?! No one even makes phone calls anymore!"

I closed my eyes, unable to bear rubbernecking this car wreck.

"Yeah, you're right. I'll probably text her for our first date. Add some emojis and shit."

"You'll never have a true connection."

"'A *true* connection?'"

The two assholes laughed right in Les's face and he just took it. It was humiliating.

"Wow, you're not just a 'Beta,' you are the rarely-spotted: 'Omega.'"

They laughed some more while Les meekly responded.

"The what?"

I opened my eyes and stepped into the fray, I couldn't take it anymore.

"I'm not sure how we reached a point where you two dumbasses think being an asshole to women makes you an Alpha Male."

"We, uh…"

But they had no prepared response for me.

"You guys got a number, but what's your plan for a first date? You read about that on the manosphere blogs you've memorized? You just gonna go play mini golf or hit the movies? Still never tell her your name or what you do? Continue insulting her all night? Keep negging her?"

I looked to Les, dressing down the guys further but without even regarding them.

"Pick-up artists, Alpha Males, assholes. *Dorks* like those guys, Les? They only deal in the present. And that's fine if they want to *maybe* get laid tonight and tonight only. But those guys aren't thinking for the future. For a relationship, *marriage*."

"Who said we want that?"

I looked at them knowingly. "You do. God, do I know you do. Because you would never be trying so hard to be assholes in the present if you hadn't been so pathetically unlucky in finding love in the past."

On the TVs, a porn star accidentally put his penis in the wrong hole and his female co-star abruptly slapped him across his face.

The bartender returned and handed them each their orders. Two Coke Zeroes.

I noticed Erin and Cheryl had been monitoring the whole situation from afar. Seeing my chance, I grabbed Les and quickly dragged him out of Bloopers and onto Eleventh Avenue.

"What the fuck was that?"

"Wait."

"For what?"

Just then, Erin jogged out of the bar, feigning anger.

"Hey, you trying to Irish goodbye us or something?"

I looked back at her.

"Uh…no. Les just lost his phone. Call his, wouldja?"

Erin pulled out her phone and I quickly punched Les's number into it. His phone instantly began ringing and he retrieved it from his front pocket.

"Oh would you look at that! Right in your front pocket the whole time, Les! How embarrassing."

Erin smiled, onto my game.

"Now you have each other's numbers, and now Les and I can head on to another bar."

"Well you better text me when you guys get there!" Erin

kissed Les on the cheek and headed back into Bloopers.

I smiled at Les. "True Alphas aren't assholes, we just didn't give a fuck."

Les stared at his phone like it was the Holy Grail.

"So? Looks like someone has an admirer, huh?"

"Just when I was beginning to think there was no one in the world for me."

"There's someone in the world for everyone."

"Now that's not true."

"It's a big world, bud. And *everyone* has admirers."

lesson number five
EVEN FAT ASSES HAVE ADMIRERS

Rose was a terrible name for a fat woman. There are not really any good names for fat women in today's cruel world, but Rose was the worst. Rose was a pretty name. Roses were pretty. Rose was certainly not.

Rose worked a basic office job where she wasn't paid a lot of money or attention. Certainly not from you. You weren't rude or anything. You never snickered like everyone else. Never tried taking cellphone pics of her hydraulic desk chair nearly touching the carpet every time she sat down. Never rolled your eyes at her fat rolls. Never gawked at the massive burritos she brought back to the office for lunch, the disposable tins of pay-by-the-pound pasta she purchased in the office cafeteria, the 1500-calorie lattes (really just caffeinated milkshakes) she supplemented her afternoons with. You just didn't really regard her, Les.

You never thought about Rose like you never thought about 99.9% of your coworkers. It's hard to pay attention to others when you're so caught up in your own shit. But, that can come back to bite you as I'm going to explain.

One day, do you remember, you were walking with that paralegal Jimmy and you passed Rose's cubicle. Her cubicle decorated with pictures of cats she wished she could own. Of course Rose was allergic to cats and couldn't even, health-wise, be a pathetic cat lady. After you two got a little bit past Rose's cube—other people in the office disparagingly called it Rose's sty—Jimmy smiled and noted: "What I wouldn't give to be suffocated by her!"

And you chuckled. Not because it was funny, but because you thought Jimmy was trying to be funny in that way former fratboys (James Von Ludwig, Delta Upsilon, University of Virginia, '06) often liked to joke. You didn't find these jokes funny, but you often laughed at other people's lame jokes to make them feel you were part of their club. Even if you didn't care to be.

Oddly enough, though, Jimmy wasn't joking, and thus your feigned chuckle was uncalled for, if not downright rude. And he noticed.

"I'm serious, man! I'd fuck her so long she'd get toxic shock syndrome!"

So now you probably felt like a jerk, both for laughing at Jimmy for claiming he wanted to have carnal relations with Rose, and for laughing at Rose because you thought Jimmy was joking and would never want to have carnal relations with someone like Rose. Les, haven't you learned you would always be better off just being yourself?

Jimmy told me all about this at your company Christmas party last year. No surprise, Jenn hadn't been able to attend, and you, not wanting to squander your plus-one, had invited me. Which made people plus-wonder if you were gay. I hope you've lived that down by now.

You probably assumed Jimmy's admiration for Rose was a novelty thing. Like Jimmy was a perv with some sexual checklist with boxes he wanted to check off to impress the other bros he drank with after work. But after speaking with him, I'm certain his heart is pure even if his dick is not.

But this isn't a story about Jimmy. This is a story about that cute secretary of yours, Chelsey. I know you hate pawning off your menial work on another person, especially a woman, but Chelsey is pretty great. Although, she wasn't exactly shy about telling me your secrets. Like those mysterious boxes that kept arriving for you. Yes, I know.

"Another?" you'd say.

"Another," Chelsey would note, with twinkled amusement in her eyes.

You'd dig your hands into some packing peanuts and remove yet another stuffed teddy bear with a note on it: "Squeeze me." And so you would, the robotic bear coming to life and talking, a microtape clearly hidden in its fur like those creepy Teddy Ruxpins briefly popular in the late-'80s.

"Hi Lesley…you have a secret admirer!" they always said and you'd always look at Chelsey, shaking your head.

"I hate this crap."

"I know, boss."

"Why doesn't this person just reveal themselves?"

"Maybe she—or he…"

"Oh God."

"—is scared."

"She—or he—should be."

"Why? 'Cause you're a homophone?"

"Homophobe."

"Gonna kick some ass?"

"You know me better than that. I almost hired a homosexual."

"But you didn't. You hired me. Why?"

"'Cause…uh…you aren't a homosexual."

I know, you would have preferred to have hired a man, but the only men interested in the secretarial job were gay or African-American and you certainly didn't want that. You just wanted a privileged heterosexual white male from a good college to boss around, not some minority. Or female.

"That doesn't make you look good."

"Not what I meant."

"I'm kidding. I know what a homophone is. Those pink

Blackberries my gay friends use, right?"

"No, I just meant…he or she is lucky I don't rat them out to HR."

"Why would you? I think this whole thing is romantical."

"'Romantical?'"

"Something better than romantic."

"Romantical."

"Exactly. So you wanna do some sleuthing or what? I'm gonna call the bear company."

From what I understand, office doors are never closed at Henderson Networth, unless someone is getting fired, or fucked, or encouraged to fuck so as to not get fired (have you heard those rumors, bud?). So there was obviously some tittering around the office when you closed your door with your hot, young secretary inside. Most people figured there was a 90% chance she came out crying. Or walking funny.

But, actually, the mere act of you closing your office door with your hot secretary inside probably could have done some of the sleuthing work for you. Because, if this secret admirer sat anywhere near your office, her—or his—head would surely be spinning by now, and the next time you saw this person they would surely act like a bitch—or a dick—to you.

"I bet it's that gross lug Tina," you told Chelsey.

"Yeah, she is kinda gross."

"She's always telling me about her newest underwear purchases. 'And I just picked up these satin lace-ups that are soooo sexy.'"

"She talks to everyone like that."

"She does?!"

"And, yes, it is gross."

Someone finally picked up the phone at Teddy's Furry Friends and Chelsey held up her hand, shushing you.

"Yes, so it could have been purchased at any one of three locations? OK, transfer me to the first."

"Maybe my admirer is that divorcée in accounting."

"Chrissy?!"

"Remember when she kept trying to dance with me at that one conference?"

"You were shitfaced! She wasn't dancing with you, she was trying to prevent you from toppling over."

"You haven't sold one of those this week? OK, transfer me..."

"Ooh...well what about that knockout in guest services? She's always using blatant double entendres around me. 'Would you like me to sharpen your pencil?'"

"She's the office girl. She sharpens pencils...and gets you pens, notepads, etcetera."

"Are you sure?!"

"Hi. Yes. Yes. Correct." Chelsey laughed into the phone. "OK, thanks."

"What is it?!"

"I now know who your secret admirer is."

"It was Tina, right? Tina?"

"It's Lawrence."

"The security guy?!"

"Uh hm."

"What the fuck?! Last time I shoot the shit about the Knicks with him."

"Slow down. The teddies were meant for Leslie Carmichael. That pretty new paralegal who sits next to Jimmy."

I died laughing at the end of Chelsey's story as she went off to the bathroom. I stood at the office party bar by myself, watching you schmooze with Jimmy, utterly clueless. I looked across the floor and saw Lawrence the security guy having a blast dancing amongst a group of younger women, all treating him like some father figure. None of them having any clue he had ulterior motives towards their friend Leslie Carmichael, cute as a button, well worth admiring.

So, I focused my attention on her. I could tell she was nervous around her new officemates, and when she came to the bar for her next cosmo, I introduced myself.

"So I've heard you're quite the talk of this office. Been receiving a zoo's worth of teddy bears, huh?"

"How do you know?"

"I don't work in this office. So everyone tells me everything."

Leslie explained how, that day after you found out the gifts were meant for her, how you had walked all of them back over to her desk. You'd quickly explained the situation to her, noting how there had been a huge mix-up. And then you hadn't even stuck around her desk long enough to see her reaction, quickly retreating back to your own office. Leslie assumed you didn't want to embarrass her, which made her think you were even a better guy than she had already assumed. Because, you see, as Leslie told me that night, with such a sad look on her face:

"It didn't work, Devin."

"'Didn't work?' What do you mean?"

Leslie exhaled, forcing a smile at me.

"My trick. It got your friend Les to come over to my desk. But it didn't work."

◉ Sandbar (w. 49th and Tenth Ave.) | 12:25 AM

chapter nine

WHAT DON'T MOST MEN UNDERSTAND: SHE LIKES YOU!?

"NO!"

"Yes."

"That can't be true!"

"It is."

"Why didn't you tell me?!??!"

"I just did."

"*Then.*"

"You were dating Jenn."

"Not at *that* party I wasn't."

"But in *that* life you were."

I looked around the bar while Les gathered his thoughts. It was dark, lit only by faux-tiki torches, really just lamps with cheap wood paneling around them.

"I had such a crush on Leslie! Why didn't you tell me this, asshole?"

"You would have left Jenn? To shit where you eat with Leslie?!"

Les thought about it, his head spinning.

"Well…FUCK, man. Now Leslie is dating…"

"Jimmy."

"Yeah, I know."

Aaron Goldfarb | 101

"I guess he didn't really admire Rose."

"Just, fuck. Thanks for being a friend."

I'd been holding onto this secret for a while. This had been the perfect time to tell him.

"Forget it, bud. A Lesley-Leslie relationship would have just been too bizarre."

If hearing his longtime crush actually had a *quid pro crush* didn't breathe some life into him, then nothing else would tonight.

"You don't know that!"

We stood in silence for the length of a song. Across the room, the dance "sand" was filling up with young dipshits and the kinds of women who didn't think they were. The women barely paid attention to the men as they all took pictures of themselves then loaded them onto Instagram. That's all people did when they went out nowadays.

"Look at those girls over there. 'So what you'd do on Friday?' 'Oh not much, just went to the bar and did mobile uploads all night.' They're stuck seeing life through filters."

"No shit. And Facebook?"

"Lot of pictures of ugly babies, huh? Kids are going to be really pissed when they're old enough to realize every single photo ever taken of them since they came out their mom's slit is currently online."

"Have you checked out some of the old people from high school?"

"No. I *like* myself."

Les looked down at me. "Come on."

"*Occasionally*."

"I don't mean the cool people, though. Although, it is interesting to see how un-cool they've become."

"How fucking gross is Matty Sanders?!"

"The prom king..."

"...Now the Burger King."

"But look at the profiles of the hugest losers. The band geeks, AP Calc nerds, flag corps dweebs...those people are not just as ugly as you recall. They're worse!"

Les was starting to annoy me with his whining.

"But then I always check out their relationship statuses..."

I gave him a frustrated, "Go ahead" eye bulge.

"*Married.*"

I wondered if he thought that was supposed to blow my mind.

"All these losers are married! To a man. To a woman. They are not just in relationships, but they are *married*! And most have kids!"

"So?"

"How can that be?"

I was confused.

"They're all married to ugly losers, right?"

"Well, yeah."

"Sooo...let me get this straight, Les. You're jealous 350-pound former tuba player Will Cimino is now married to a whale? You wish you had a wife so big that when you spoon it ends up looking like a Venn diagram?!"

"No." He paused. "Of course not."

"Then, what are you bitching about?"

"I'm bitching they've found love and I haven't!"

"You have."

"I *could have* had it with Jenn or Leslie or..."

"Huh? You could have had Leslie if you'd just nutted up and talked to her."

He was barely listening to me anymore, so lost in his self-loathing.

"I'm not that great looking a guy. I do all right, but I'm certainly not that rich. Or that famous."

"You're not any percentage famous."

"Exactly! I'm Z-list!"

"You're not on *the* list. *Any* of them."

"You're crushing me, man!"

"Look at things from another perspective, bud. Maybe people like Will Cimino are blessed in a way we never will be.

Maybe these ugly, fat, uninteresting, dumb, boring fucks don't have any false ambitions they could snag someone amazing. So, instead, they take whomever they can get, which, of course, is someone as similarly lacking in positive qualities as them."

"I guess."

"It's not *a* guess. It's true. It's the same with high school sweethearts who end up together. A total lack of ambition."

I put my arm on his back and scooted closer.

"People like you and me, people who actually have things going for them, only we could be dumb enough to think we have the goods to snag the most amazing woman on this planet."

"It's a curse."

"It is. But it's also a blessing. You just have to be brutally honest with yourself."

A group of loud girls came back from the bar carrying a giant fish bowl full of some neon green liquid, a dozen hot pink straws shoved into the concoction.

"Look, man, I have this friend Steve. We hang out at that whiskey bar across the street occasionally. Steve spends a lot of time at bars because he has a startup for honeytrapping. You know what that is?"

"Like…beekeepers? Wear those meshy astronaut suits, shoot smoke everywhere?"

"Not exactly. Steve prefers bespoke suits from this guy in Tribeca. No, what Steve does is test people's integrity."

"What does that mean?"

"Husbands and boyfriends who suspect their significant others may be cheating hire Steve. He then figures out when and where these folks' wives and girlfriends are going to be alone—maybe at the park, or a store, or usually a bar—and then he goes and…well, he hits on them."

"Then what?"

The fishbowl girls put their heads together, each wrapped their bloated lips around a straw, and sucked. The air left the room.

"Then he sees what happens. Does the wife remain uninterested or does she flirt back?"

"And…?"

"And that's how he traps honey. How he proves your partner is unfaithful."

Les looked repulsed. "Does Steve have…sex with them?"

"Sometimes he has to! As *proof*."

Les tried to wrap his head around a world he hadn't even known existed.

"Steve must be good looking though. I mean, if he was talking up someone like Rose who's never been with any one… *attractive*, it just wouldn't be fair."

"Exactly! That's why Steve has to first figure out how attractive the target honey is, then only send a trapper at that same level."

"OK…"

"Steve's a 5. *Average*. Thus, he's only allowed to go out and trap *average* women. Luckily for him and his business, there are many average women out there. Look around the bar, Les, numbers will appear over the head of every woman you see…"

"Of course, Steve employs honeytrappers from all ends of the spectrum. He's got this stinky 300-pound guy who's his '1.' He also has this Hugh Jackman lookalike who goes after the truly gorgeous women. Models and actresses. Or musclebound gay men. Gay men hire Steve a lot. They *always* suspect infidelity."

I took a sip from my Mai Tai. It tasted like Kool-Aid without a hint of booze. If anything was to blame for tomorrow's hangover, it would be this shit.

"Les, you need to be like Steve in assessing yourself. Figure out exactly what you are. Then go after *those* women."

"And what if those women are not what I want?"

"Then *improve* yourself."

I turned Les to face the wall and a fingerprint-covered mirror.

"Look at yourself and think about what you are on a ten-point scale. A number will immediately come to your head…"

"6 point 5."

That's what everyone usually said. Les needed to drink some more so his self-beer goggles kicked in and he got more confidence.

"Not bad."

"But is that good enough to get Erin? She must be…" He thought about it. "…a 7 point 5. Shit."

"You can get her."

"It's just so hard for me to know…if a girl *likes* me."

I started cracking up. "Les, you sound like a seven-year-old. Come on, bud. Women are not that complex. You've heard of Ockham's Razor?"

"I'm surprised you have."

"Wikipedia, baby. It's like a one-night stand with knowledge."

"True enough."

"So, tell me Les, what is Ockham's Razor?"

"The explanation for *anything* is usually the simplest reason. So…?"

"So anything positive a girl says to you, probably means she likes you. She wouldn't be speaking to you otherwise. On an elementary school playground, a little girl sprints up to a little boy. 'Tag, you're it!' *She likes him.*

"A teenage girl leans across the aisle and tells a boy she's having trouble with the Periodic Table. Could he help her out? *She likes him*!

"A high schooler invites her male 'friend' over to watch TV. Halfway through she starts shivering and gets a blanket, even though it's a warm night. 'You can get under it with me if you'd like.' *She fucking likes him*!"

I nodded toward a man and woman sitting in the corner, sharing a coconut with two curly straws in it.

"Two adults drink at a bar. The woman notes, 'Oh, you like *The Hangover*? I just got it on Blu-Ray, let's go back to my place and watch it.' *She fucking likes him*! And wants to fucking fuck him."

The man awkwardly leaned across the table, putting his hand on the woman's forearm as she said something to him.

"Quit picking daisies and pulling petals. 'She likes me, she likes me not. She wants to fuck me, she wants to fuck me not.' Fuck that! She *does*. And she fucking *will*! Here, give me your phone."

Les handed me his phone and before he had a chance to stop me, I sent a text to Erin.

"It's like I need to literally hold your dick and insert it. From now on, bud, just assume if a woman is *willingly* talking to you…then she likes you."

"You're right. I know you're right. It's just…women can be so hard to understand, Devin. If only there was any easier way to know what they want."

"There is. Because they all want the same thing."

"What's that?"

"You ever watch…chick flicks?"

Les stared at me curiously.

"Hell yes *I* watch them, bud. Because chick flicks show you how women think relationships are *supposed* to work."

"Aren't chick flicks written by gay dudes?"

"I don't think so…uh…maybe. Doesn't matter. All that matters is they are voraciously consumed by straight women."

"*YOU* watch chick flicks?"

"I used to."

"Which ones?"

"All the ones. *10 Things I Hate About You* and *How to Lose a Guy in 10 Days*. *27 Dresses* and *13 Going on 30* and *50 First Dates*. *Pretty Woman* and *Bride Wars*. *Flashdance* and *Dirty Dancing* and *Save the Last Dance*. *New Year's Eve* and *Leap Year* and *Valentine's Day* and everything and anything with Ryan Gosling. I'm eternally grateful to Nora Ephron. R.I.P."

"This is maybe the most shocking thing you've ever told me."

"Man, when I was younger, twelve dollars, a box of Sour Patch Kids and a few smuggled tallboys…then just two hours of my life got me so much insight into the female mind."

Aaron Goldfarb | 107

I'd sit in the theater, the lights would dim, and soon the title would splash across the screen in massive Helvetica…

lesson number six

A MAN CAN LEARN FROM CHICK FLICKS

Andy (Bradley Cooper, sporting a new haircut that was the topic of a lead story on Entertainment Tonight) and his friends (that short guy from *The League*, that black guy from *30 Rock*, and that dude you once saw do stand-up on *Jimmy Fallon*) take bong rips as strippers dance in front of them.

The strippers aren't naked, just in bras and panties so as to not turn off the female audience. Also, to help shill a new high-tech brassiere that is gratuitously product-dropped when one scantily-clad woman says to another: "Aren't these Victoria's Secret AbracadaBras™ *uuuuh*-mazing?!"

"Being single is awesome!" Andy shouts to Chuck (black guy, *30 Rock*) who offers a fist pound and lamely adds "Bingo bang-o!" like the screenwriters intended it to become a catch phrase. Female audience members are supposed to be turned off by the Andy character, though they can't help but enjoy Bradley Cooper's dreamy cobalt eyes, while ignoring the rumors of his homosexuality prevalent in the blogosphere.

The next scene, played under the opening credits, takes place at Ralph's, a supermarket chain not actually in Brooklyn, where this film is set. A clearly hungover Andy places a six-pack of Coors Lite (product placement), a handle of vodka (generic), and a case of Trojan condoms (logo obscured) on the conveyer belt, using a Slim Jim (product placement) as his item separator. "Just the essentials," he smirks to cashier Betty White.

Off-screen, a voice we recognize notes: "*Essentially* disgusting."

It's Kate (Reese Witherspoon) and women in the audience titter, eager with anticipation for the story to kick into rom-com gear.

With a shit-eating grin, Andy responds: "Sounds like you wanna join me."

"Not in a million years, buddy," snaps Kate, and the female audience members pump their fists, recalling the most recent bad boy in their own lives. "Paper or plastic?" adds Betty White.

"Why so angry?" wonders Andy. "*Plastic*." Because, as we will soon learn, Kate turns thirty the next day and is still single. People will later go to Reese Witherspoon's IMDB page to investigate her real age.

Kate overshares: "I frequently am a bridesmaid at weddings of friends uglier than me. And no men will date me except for bald, neurotic losers."

As they both exit the grocery store, Andy lobs a grenade: "Have you considered that's because you're kinda a miserable bitch?"

Andy says exactly what the few heterosexual men who will ever see this movie are thinking, but the line isn't meant for them. The white women in the audience cover their mouths in shock, "ethnic" women go "Ooooooooooooooh!," and the homosexual men histrionically snap at the screen.

"I've never considered that because I have no self-awareness," Kate wails—and Andy's facade is cracked. We finally see some heart and start to like him.

"I'm sorry to upset you. Here, have a beer and relax," says Andy, ripping a Coors Lite (the label clearly facing the camera) from the six-pack ring. Kate hesitantly accepts and…

…the less-than-accomplished filmmaking team behind previous efforts *Boyenemy* and *The One* opts to smash cut to that night at a bar without offering any sort of reasonable plot development for how they got from there to here because, honestly, the filmmakers don't have any clue how these kinds of things happen.

Kate now dances on top of the bar—one that looks nothing like any bar any audience member has ever drank in—having stripped down to just a white tank top. [Production stills showing an accidental nip slip have already leaked to the internet, going viral after Mr. Skin posts them. Cynics presume these were intentionally leaked to add to the marketing buzz for the movie. It works as the opening weekend rakes in $25M despite a 34% "fresh" rating on Rotten Tomatoes.]

"I never drink this much!" Kate screams as she stage dives off the bar and into Andy's arms.

Side-wipe to Andy's bachelor pad where he and Kate have sex, her on top, also wearing the new Victoria's Secret AbracadaBra. On her exaggerated orgasm, the filmmakers opt for a more subtle fade to black and then fade up from black for the next scene, which begins with the sound of Foleyed birds chirping. Our amazing understanding of cinematic language allows us to deduce…it's morning.

Both Andy and Kate wake up simultaneously. Andy arrogantly smiles. A freaked-out Kate touches her chest to make sure she's still dressed. She isn't, though we don't see anything and the film maintains a PG-13 rating.

"*What* did we do last night?!"

"Would you like to see the videotape?" Andy says with a smirk, though we assume he's kidding. Now female audience members go back to hating Bradley Cooper, fuck his cobalt eyes and hot abs. A moment of calm comes over Kate, and she prudently notes:

"Since we just had sex, you now have to be my boyfriend."

"Sure, I'll sleep with you again!" Andy yells over his shoulder back toward the bedroom as he loudly urinates with the door ajar, scratching his impressively toned buttocks (presumably a double). Kate has a stunned, frustrated look on her face. And now we realize, the entire plot of this movie: taming this sexy beast.

As the second act begins, a few days later—noted by a graphic on screen, the filmmakers not completely trusting our intelligence—Andy puts on a rumpled suit and tie. Meanwhile, Andy's friends drink more product placement beer—the new Coors Lite Unreasonably Cold—as they play video games.

"Why you got on a suit, bro?"

"Yeah. You look like a fag."

Andy actually looks perturbed. [GLAAD was also perturbed and the previous line was eventually cut before the movie went nationwide.]

"I got my first real date with Kate tonight and she told me to dress up."

"Yeah, well you're gonna miss a lot of fun. Chuck just got the new *Aliens versus Zombies* Xbox game."

That night, at a fancy restaurant, Andy and Kate quietly dine.

"I can't believe you have such a carefree lifestyle," she remarks.

"Yeah, it's pretty great."

"Well I don't like it one bit, Andy. I'm going to make you

miserable and crush your dreams."

And she does, in montage-form, cross-cut with scenes of Andy's friends playing *Aliens versus Zombies*, an odd directorial choice:

First, Kate makes Andy hang out with her nagging friends and their loser husbands.

Then she makes him go shopping with her and watch as she tries on outfit after outfit.

Finally, Kate makes Andy wear clothes he hates. Stuff you have to tuck in. Stuff with pleats and tassels.

"Next we'll get your hair cut and shave that stubble. You have to become boyfriend material."

Meanwhile, all of Andy's friends wear football jerseys, heading out to watch the big playoff game, harassing Andy.

"Dude, I cannot believe you aren't going!"

"Your favorite team is playing!"

"You haven't missed a game in, like, ten years!"

Andy looks like he's about to cry.

"My girlfriend won't even give me four hours a week to do what I want."

"And you're too big of a pussy to tell her otherwise?"

Or, at least, an unrealistic script has made him that way, almost overnight.

One of his friends, the short guy from *The League*, curiously examines Andy's scalp, making the audience nervously laugh, and also causing us to think this guy will soon be a break-out star a la Zach Galifianakis's supporting work in *The Hangover*.

"Is there gel in your hair?"

"I think it's mousse."

"Oh, it's *mooooooooooooooousse?*" he says in an intentionally humorous way, a line many men in the audience can't help repeating for the next few weeks.

That night, Andy and Kate snuggle and watch *The Notebook*, another property from the Warner Bros. library, synergistically coming out with a ten-year anniversary Blu-Ray edition box set ($49.99) that very week.

"Can you believe I'm so controlling I made you skip your beloved football game when we didn't even have concrete plans?"

"It would be one thing if we were going to a wedding or a business dinner or something important."

"I know! But I'm such a bitch I won't even let you have a fun four hours with the boys!"

Andy sighs. Most women in the audience side with Kate. They eat this shit up. If only *they* could control *their* men so easily. Yeah, perhaps if you looked like Reese Witherspoon does in an AbracadaBra.

"Can we at least check the score?"

Kate leans forward on the sofa and looks Andy right in the eye.

"Not. A. Chance."

(That line will become an oft-repeated catchphrase that women love to ambiguously post as Facebook status updates and watch the "likes" flow in from their female friends while their clueless male friends comment, "'Not a chance'…what???")

That night, in her darkened bedroom only lit by the glow of the TV, while Kate sleeps, Andy watches on mute the *SportsCenter* highlights of his favorite team's victory that night. His friends appear in the highlights giving each other high-fives next to an empty seat where Andy would have been sitting.

"I've just had an end-of-the-second-act epiphany!" screams Andy. And the third act begins with another smash cut to Andy proudly marching into the bar, still in his bathrobe, a nice bit of comic relief in an otherwise tense scene. His buddies turn and smile. "Look who it is!"

"Are you sleepwalking?" the guy from *The League* cracks, "Because there's no way such a whipped man like you would possibly be at this bar."

"Being single again is awesome!"

And everybody does a "cheers" to that!

A few days later, according to another graphic, Kate cries on a friend's shoulder while another friend consoles her. These are the same friends from previous montages and this is known as the "Our Hero is Nearly Defeated" portion of a three-act screenplay structure.

"You were too good for him."

"He was too hard to control too!"

Through sobs, Katie agrees. So does the audience. But, they can't help but wish things had turned out better because Bradley Cooper is just so damn hot.

"I tried to make his life as miserable as possible. Why did he leave me?!"

Meanwhile, one of the smoking hot girls from the opening scene is all over Andy at the bar, as the filmmakers employ some uneven cross-cutting techniques.

"We are potentially going to have a one-night stand, right?"

The girl coquettishly smiles at Andy.

"Replace 'potentially' with '*absolutially*!'"

Andy looks concerned, and not just by her made-up word.

"What? Did I say something wrong?"

"No, Destiny, it's not you, it's just…yes, you're tons hotter than Kate and much cooler too. You actually drink and you like my friends and they like you and you clearly aren't controlling and you seem to love sex and football too and you are an independent women and you're so awesome…"

"But…?"

"But…I'm an idiot that can't get that miserable wench I used to date off my mind."

"Then I'm going to do what no girl in the history of the world has ever done before and say: 'Go after her!'"

Andy smiles, kisses Destiny chastely on the cheek, and sprints from the bar. His friends laugh.

"He is hopeless!"

"Hopelessly in love!"

"Lucky bastard!" says the guy from *The League* as we clearly realize his snarky ways mask an inner desire to also be loved.

Andy sprints through the dark streets as it pours rain, the bright lights of the big city reflecting off the ground. The female audience is starting to get excited too. They can feel a happy ending near, but the filmmakers are still going to make them work a little for it. And, as we are at the 120 minute mark, it better come soon because I have to really take a leak from the Tecates I've been pounding.

Meanwhile, we return to Kate's apartment where she sleeps on the couch under an afghan, a box of tissues nearby, a finished tub of product-placement Edy's Lo-Cal Brownie Mix ice cream on the coffee table. The doorbell rings and she wakes up, confused. She calls out: "Who is it?"

"It's me."

Kate is shocked. And quickly tries to make herself presentable.

"Go away! I don't want to see you!"

"I got something to say!" Andy shouts from behind the door.

Kate quickly grabs a toothbrush and brushes her teeth vigorously. Spritzes on some perfume. Fixes her hair.

"I don't wanna hear it!"

"Just give me a second!" Andy hollers through the mail slot, adding a bit of hijinks.

Finally presentable, Kate opens the door to see a drenched Andy.

"Fine!"

She taps her toe on the ground angrily.

"Spill it."

Andy is out of breath, his wet boyfriend-material hair cascading over his cobalt eyes. Bradley Cooper has never looked sexier.

"I'm an idiot. You weren't controlling me. You were right! You're the best thing that's ever happened to me. Will you take me back?"

"Do you cede any and all power you have to me?"

"Absolutely."

"Can I put your balls in a vise and squeeze for the next sixty years?"

"Wouldn't have it any other way."

"And you'll never leave me again?"

Andy smirks.

"Not. A. Chance."

Kate wraps her arms around Andy, kissing him passionately as the camera takes several 360-degree laps around them.

The majority of the movie theater audience erupts with joy, but the few heterosexual men on dates look distraught.

Their female dates look toward them, lovingly digging their hands into their upper thighs, mere inches from their testicles. They clench tightly. And smile.

📍 **J. Mac's** (w. 57th and Eleventh Ave.) | 1:31 AM

chapter ten

WHAT DO WOMEN WANT

"As you can see, Les, if a man is living his life like the male lead in a chick flick, he needs to start doing the complete opposite of that."

"That is such garbage!" Erin scoffed at me. She and Cheryl had met up with us after I had texted them on Les's phone. I'd even added an emoji. Women seemed to like them.

"Chick flicks are female porn."

"What does that even mean?!"

"It's fantasy. You're not really attracted to the kind of weenies presented as the male species in chick flicks. You just like the concept of a hunky man fawning all over you. You wouldn't like it in execution."

"Yeah, being fawned over would be *awful*." Erin tried to mock me.

"And now you're acting like the kind of oblivious woman who is often the lead character in chick flicks."

I smiled, but not for long. It looked like Erin might punch me in the face.

Cheryl spoke up. "Yeah, I agree with Devin. Chick flicks make me wish I didn't have a vagina."

I casually put my arm around Cheryl, bringing her in close. "That's funny, because just earlier Les was wishing he didn't have a dick!"

I laughed and Cheryl joined me. Les sheepishly put in his two cents for Erin's benefit. "I, uh, believe Devin is quoting me out of context."

Erin looked toward Les's crotch, raising her eyebrows.

It began to drizzle as we passed CBS Studios—giant billboards promoting their fall lineup, *Two Broke Girls*, *Two Old Farts*, *Two and a Half More Men*—before turning west on 57th Street and entering a dead part of town packed with car dealerships, storage facilities, warehouses, and probably whorehouses too.

Halfway down the street, I opened the door to a scuzzy-looking dive, J. Mac's. If Rudy's had made Drunx look like the 21 Club, J. Mac's made Rudy's look like Le Cirque. Cheryl, Erin, and Les hesitantly looked at each other as I soldiered inside. As it was becoming the wee hours of the night, the bar was now empty, just a few old men teetering on battered barstools. There were probably no hours at this joint that were considered "happy," but this time was downright depressing.

"I think it's actually working, Devin," Les whispered to me.

"Working?"

"Yeah. Erin just asked me what my response would be if she said she wanted to get XXX with me. She said that: 'X!X!X!'"

Les poked me in gut with each repeated mention of "X," before smiling wide.

"So…?"

"I think she wants a triple-X porno hookup."

I nodded. He was drunk. "Yeah. Maybe."

We walked the length of the bar, looking for the closest-to-clean spot to place our asses. The joint had no beer taps, just icy longnecks in a cooler, their labels peeling off, a few stray bottles of rotgut on a shelf, and dust caked on everything. Fluorescent lights brighter than a suburban Wal-Mart's illuminated the craggy faces staring back at us.

"COULD YOU KIDS FIND A FUCKIN' SEAT?!"

An old crank in a U.S. Marines hat spun on his stool.

"DON'T TALK TO THE CUSTOMERS LIKE THAT!" The woman behind the bar swatted down the old man's bill, knocking it over his eyes. She had beefy forearms and a wisp of a mustache. She looked at us and offered a kind smile. "Now what can I getcha kids?"

"Your four coldest beers."

"They'll be from the absolute bottom of the cooler, hon."

We slid into a filthy booth and Les set his rain-soaked cardboard box in the middle of the table like a centerpiece. Someone had dumped bar peanuts into it at one of our recent stops.

"Seriously, it's time to dump that box, bud. Or donate it to some of the transients in here."

"Don't rush him. He can do it when he's ready," Erin responded.

"Are you ready?" I asked her.

"For what?" She went on the defensive.

"Men. *Again*."

Erin laughed, trying to mask her fear.

"You should tell them about your last date," Cheryl prodded her friend.

Erin rolled her eyes. "Oh God."

"What happened?" Les feigned extreme curiosity because he thought women liked when you did that.

"Well…it was the first and *only* date I've had since my breakup. It was with this guy…let's call him Bryan…

* * *

Let's Call Him Bryan was carrying a wicker picnic basket when I met up with him at Central Park. One of those pricey ones you get at Williams-Sonoma. I sure hoped he had borrowed it from someone who had gotten it as a gift from someone they didn't really like, who blew lots of money on gifts for people they barely knew.

"D'you remember who I was when I texted?" he asked.

"Of course." (*"No. Dozens of dorks ask for my number when I go out drinking."*)

"I was worried you wouldn't respond. Guess I impressed?"

"Absolutely!" (*Or...I had nothing to do today.*)

"I thought Central Park would be romantic for our first date."

"What a great choice!" (*Because nothing says romance like the smell of hansom cab horse shit, the sight of bumbling tourists, the sounds of mediocre street performers...*)

Bryan reached out to grab my hand and I hesitantly acquiesced.

"—" (*...and the touch of a clammy paw.*)

I looked down and noted...

"Oooh, manly hands." (*Wow, those are small. Can you even grip a football?*)

"You know what they say about hand size, heh heh. And the motion of the ocean."

"That is hilarious." (—)

"This date wasn't completely my idea. My ex-girlfriend-I'm-still-friends-with suggested it."

"Good call!" (*"Do you understand she doesn't want you to get laid?"*)

"She suggested the picnic basket too. $200. Williams Sonoma."

"How sweet!" (*Oh yeah. She's totally trying to block your cock.*)

"Open the basket, you can help me set the 'table.' Ha ha."

"What a spread!" (*I'm never gonna spread 'em. "Where the fuck is the wine?!"*)

"If you're looking for wine, I just read in Men's Health you shouldn't drink on a first date because, #1, you don't want to give the impression you have to drink to have a good time..."

"—" (*"It's not an impression."*)

"...and, #2, you could end up in bed with someone before both of you are truly ready..."

That was my last straw and led to me discreetly activating

Aaron Goldfarb | 121

my Text Me Outta Here app.

"...and I know they say 'in vino veritas,' wine brings truth..."

Which caused my iPhone to make the iconic bloop text message notification sound some thirty seconds later.

"...but doesn't it really just bring hangovers, vomiting, and poor decisions?

Which led to me pulling my phone from my purse and feigning shock when I saw the message from Text Me Outta Here, a randomized text that gave someone a feasible excuse for a date escape:

"Oh my god! I'm so sorry, Bryan, but...apparently, my... roommate's suicidal cat is caught in a tree. I need to go help her talk him down!" (*Best 99 cent app I've ever bought!*)

Let's Call Him Bryan acted overly concerned and, of course, asked "Can I see you again?" which I, of course, replied,

"Of course." (*"Get real."*)

I never saw him again. He finally gave up texting me three weeks later.

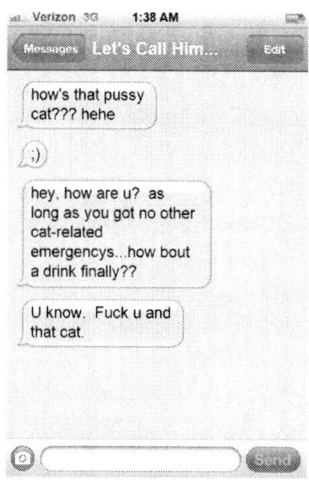

* * *

The bartender came over to our booth with four beer bottles held in her hands in a diamond shape and, in a cigarette-smoke growl informed me, "Twenty dah-lers, hon." Les, of course, paid her as she added, "And don't worry about him," nodding toward the old crank. "He's just the owner. PHIL, QUIT TRYING TA' SCARE YER CUST-A-MAHS."

"Thank you, Erin, for helping me teach Les."

"Teach him what?"

I looked at Les. "Teach him that you shouldn't listen to a single damn thing women say."

"What?"

"Your words are worthless."

"My words?" Erin looked disgusted at me.

"A woman's words." I turned back toward Les. "Instead, you pay attention to what she does."

Les looked toward Erin. "She's currently balling up her fist, Devin."

Aaron Goldfarb | 123

I turned back to monitor Erin as I continued, "How often does she contact you? Initiate things. Touch you, hug you, kiss you, fuck you? Her behavior around you, and toward you, is so much more important than anything she could ever say to you."

"That's so not true."

"But it is, Erin. Even the words you're currently saying to me are worthless, because your actions clearly show me you're pissed."

"So…what did that guy do wrong on Erin's date?" Les pathetically looked toward her, and she finally broke contact with me to actually smile at him.

"Let's Call Him Bryan was uninteresting, unoriginal, supplicating, placating, showed no confidence, mentioned an ex, implied sex, and didn't bring wine."

"OK…but I kinda agree about not drinking on a first date. You don't?"

"God no!" the other three of us at the booth shouted at the same time.

"Les, the *only* time women say what they mean is when they're drunk. Then that ambiguity goes right out the window and they'll tell you things they wouldn't tell their diary sober. *In vino veritas*, 'Wine brings truth.' Yup, and cosmos bring crazy fucking candor."

Erin stood.

"For once, you are actually right, Devin. I am drunk. So now I will say exactly what I mean: *you* are an asshole."

She turned and headed toward the bathroom.

I looked toward Les. "Of course, when women are drunk you can listen to what they say, but now you *can't* accept what they actually *do*. Especially if it involves some freaky sex position that ain't ever happening sober, bud."

Cheryl shook her head at me. I thought she might have been at least somewhat amused by my antics. She focused in on Les.

"Les, women will *say* they want a date at a fancy restaurant where the man brings roses and jewelry…" Cheryl paused.

"Sure, and I'm certain an awesome first date for a guy would be playing eighteen holes while his date caddied."

"Hand me my lob wedge, honey!" I yelled. "Ooh, that does sound nice. You interested in the job, Cher?" She ignored me.

"But that wouldn't lead to love. It might not even lead to her nineteenth hole. But, just like Erin, I too recall my most recent first date. It was back in January."

"January? Cold spell, huh?" I tweaked her.

"Not quite." Cheryl smiled pleasantly to herself. "Because that first date was actually pretty perfect…"

Les and I both perked up.

"We went to the kind of bar most men would never dream of taking me to. Most men in my past have taken me to expensive, Michelin-starred restaurants and said things they thought would impress me. Shit like: 'Many restaurants have *wagyu* beef, sure, but this is actual Japanese kobe.' Who gives a shit?!

"This bar had some TVs but not too many, some music but it wasn't too loud. It was a nice wooden bar with certainly nothing scratched into the wood, a decent food menu, decent beer menu, decent wine menu. Nothing needs to be that mind-blowing, but at least one thing should be. Just to give you something to talk about. This particular bar had their own infused liquors, housed in big vats on the wall.

"Most men choose a table for dates, but he marched us straight to the bar. Perfect! Tables ruin intimacy.

"If you have the perfect environment, now you just: Add a man. Add a woman. Add some alcohol. And mix.

"We drank and talked, drank and talked, and…things just took care of themselves. We rarely had lulls in the conversation, but any brief ones were handled by making fun of fellow bar patrons. Like this redhead that looked like a drunk Ronald McDonald. We called him Bottled McDrunkald.

"You see, Les, this kind of date has no expectations. And alcohol breaks the ice faster than a fat kid on skates. It also speeds things up. By night's end, you know *exactly* how you feel about each other. Whether you loathe her, just want to fuck him, you like her, would like to see him again, or…just want to make out sloppily on the street like high school kids."

Cheryl smiled.

"I certainly knew how I felt about *him* by the end of this first date."

I tried to show absolutely no reaction to Cheryl's revelation.

Les spoke up. "Most women say they don't even kiss on first dates, though…"

"BULLSHIT!" Cheryl snapped at him before looking toward me. "I've always figured, why waste money, time, boredom, horniness, and nerves? No matter what you've heard: *EVERY* women kisses on the first date."

"If she truly likes that first date," I added.

Cheryl winked at Les, confusing me.

"Uh…OK, I'm gonna get us some more drinks." I stood, squeezed Cheryl's shoulder, and slapped Les on the back as I headed up to the bar, sidling beside the cranky old guy.

"Marines, huh?"

"No, asshole, I just wear it for show. What da fuck do you think?"

"Should I *semper* fuck off?"

Erin returned from the bathroom, a look of revulsion on her face at what she'd just seen.

"What. A. Horror show."

"Uh…" Les tried taking charge as I watched from the bar. "How 'bout I take you out on a first date some time, Erin? To make up for Devin taking you *here*…?"

There was a pause before Cheryl and Erin started laughing at Les, just as I returned with four more beers.

"Smooth, Les."

"I didn't actually mind it," Erin noted, looking fondly at Les. "Because the best advice we can give a man is telling him to simply be himself. Warts and all. Nerdiness and neuroticism and…" She touched Les's hand. "That was sweet."

I looked back up toward the bar to see the old crank miming giving cunnilingus, an X-rated Marcel Marceau impression.

"Erin's finally right about *something*. You know when I really started having success with women?"

"When you bought a box of roofies off Amazon?" Erin snarked and I ignored her.

"It was when I quit creating phony personas to try and land them…"

lesson number seven

YOU SHOULD NEVER LIE TO WOMEN

The bright sun came in through the picture window, putting the dingy hotel room under a giant magnifying glass. The hot light tanned the four people crammed naked onto the Murphy bed from east to west: me, Tinsley, Beatrice, and Les.

The night had started out so innocuously. Les and I were starving and had gone to dinner for some churrascaria in Little Brazil. Cheryl and Erin, if you've never been to churrascaria it works like this: for a single price you get an all-you-can-eat carnivore's delight. On your table you have a card, one side is green for "go," the other is red for "stop" (serving me meat before I fall over). As numerous waiters walk the dining room carrying skewers of different meats on a stick—beef, chicken, pork, lamb, and plenty of shit wrapped in bacon—showing the green side tells them to keep piling portions onto your plates; the red side, unsurprisingly, tells them to stop. Gorging on meat without being forced to chat with service industry professionals? Sign me up!

Just one hour after dinner started, our bellies bulged like Buddha. We had easily put down a dozen pounds of animal and already listened to an endless loop of "Mas Que Nada" performed by the house bossa nova band. We'd barely even had time to talk until the check came.

"Up for a drink at Scruffy's next door?"

"I have an early meeting tomorrow, I can't drink."

"Oh, come on, Les, let's get *A* drink."

"I can't."

"Just *A* drink?"

Les thought about it.

"OK. But just *A* drink."

Nearby on Eighth Avenue was Scruffy Duffy's, a bar frequented by the bridge-and-tunnel crowd, the happy hour heroes, and flight attendants in town on layover. Perfect for a little role-playing, I thought.

"We should do our old trick tonight," I offered.

"You mean *your* old trick?"

"Sure. Whatever. OK, what should we be?"

"Why do we always have to be something?"

"Because it's fun. So what should we be?"

Les eventually acquiesced to my game, though fairly dispassionately.

"We own a series of gyms throughout the Midwest."

"Could be better."

"What could be better than owning a gym?"

"Well…what if you could drink at them?"

"Not bad. Not bad. Everyone knows the best inventions in the world are '[insert random business] and you can drink there.'"

"Then it's settled. But what are we called?"

"*Bar* Bells."

"Pumped and Drunk."

"Hmmmm…"

"It'll come…"

We reached Scruffy's to find a stream of dolled-up women being vomited out its front door. I held up the red light card I'd swiped from the Brazilian restaurant, but none stopped.

"Did a noxious gas pipe burst in back?"

I turned toward the minuscule bouncer, small as a lawn jockey, but with bulging biceps.

"Singles' speed dating event just ended," he noted in a Barry White-deep voice.

"And those are the girls no one picked up?"

The bouncer suavely laughed.

"Naw man. *No one* gets picked up at these events. Those are the ones who have a shred of dignity and want to cry about their romantic failures in the privacy of their own homes."

"So who's in the bar now?"

"What remains in the bar now, fellas, are a gaggle of desperates who didn't find 'Mr. Right' and are now content to get shitfaced while singing along to 'I Will Survive.'"

We entered Scruffy's right as several women were removing "Meet Market Adventures" signage from around the bar. Using my red light to stop traffic like a school crossing guard, we pushed our way through the failed would-be Mr. Rights. A slew of milquetoast dorks dressed for a wine tasting, clad in blazers with khakis galore, plenty of pleats, still smarting after having been collectively rebuffed. We stomped our way through the sour grapes, leaving plenty of whine in our trail as we hit the bar to get A drink.

"See anyone, Les?"

"What about them?"

I homed in on a slender woman who had just finished rolling up a large sign with another speed-dater. I held up the green light card toward the women and both actually came toward us, curious.

"Yes…?"

"You're both so law abiding."

"Thanks, but…"

"Our company had a big merger today."

"OK…"

"And…my brother…"

"Brother?"

"My brother and I would be honored if you'd have A drink

130 | *The Guide for a Single Man*

with us to celebrate."

I elbowed Les in the ribs and he pulled out his credit card, which I quickly grabbed to make sure his name remained shrouded.

"On our company, natch!"

I leaned in and extended my hand to both women.

"Hi, I'm Jason Stanton."

I looked toward Les, prodding him to say his line.

"And I'm…Johnny…Stanton."

"Yes! We're the Stanton brothers."

Back then, we often claimed we were brothers, thinking brothers seemed safer to women than two random dudes.

"You guys are really brothers?"

I grabbed Les and made him put his head next to mine, our ears nearly touching. Though we looked nothing like brothers, we simultaneously squinted our eyes and furrowed our brows. It was a classic Marx Brothers routine. Both girls scrutinized us for a few seconds before eventually smiling.

"I *do* see it!"

With 300 ccs of silicone confidence injected into her chest, I was quite jealous of Les's potential future score, this Meet Market queen bee, Beatrice. She was far too attractive to be wasting her time running dating dog and pony shows with all these donkeys and jackasses. My p.f.s., Tinsley, was cute but far too shy to flirt and do much talking. It was no wonder she'd found little success that night. I would have to break her out of her shell, push her off the wall like Humpty Dumpty. I thought I would hopefully hump her then dump her.

"I can see it…too. You both have the same…eyebrows."

It was quickly clear both these women were malleable to our every whim. Beatrice was the kind of falsely confident women that truly liked to be led, Tinsley too quiet to object. Beatrice was super talkative in that annoying "I'm outgoing" networking way, having clearly learned the "art" of conversation from a book on how to be good at conversation. She also may have also been on amphetamines, sputtering out her every word.

"So, big business deal, fellas. What's the deal? What business you guys in?"

I held up the red light, letting her know it was time to quit talking so I could get a word in.

"My brother and I run a fitness center."

"A fitness center...?"

"That you can drink at."

"That you can drink at? Why would you wanna drink at a gym?"

I smiled.

"Why *wouldn't* you?"

Tinsley shrugged.

"So what's it called?"

Les finally smiled wide and spoke a stroke of genius.

"Beer Muscles!"

I slapped him on the back with a hearty laugh.

"My brother doesn't lie. A round of shots in honor of... Beer Muscles!"

Pretty quickly, A drink became A huge bar tab and soon we were the last ones standing, just waiting for our one-night stands to begin. I must admit it, and I don't know how this had happened, but I had begun to really like Tinsley. She may have been judicious with her, uh, words, but it was clear she was sharp. She had an MBA from Penn and had even suggested some business strategies for Beer Muscles. I would have implanted them if I actually had owned a company called Beer Muscles.

"You should brand your own energy drinks. You could call each can a '$2 gym membership.'"

"Not bad. We may have to hire you as our head of marketing."

"I could be interested in that!"

With closing time approaching, and after hours no longer an after thought, I needed a place to take these girls back to. Except...we were the Stanton brothers. And the Stanton brothers weren't New York locals, according to our lies. I couldn't just take them back to my Hell's Kitchen apartment. I needed an audible.

"*Our* hotel's just a block away. Would you like to come?"

Les raised his eyebrows at me.

"Our hotel? Yes, where is our hotel…*Jason?*"

"A block away. I'm sorry, we usually stay at the…Waldorf when we come to town, but this was such a last-second trip…"

Beatrice turned.

"With all your traveling, you guys must *live* in hotels, huh?"

"Exactly. We're like Howard Hughes except we never shit our pants," Les placidly joked.

"So we'll get back to the room, hit the minibar, play some party games. And by 'party games,' I'm speaking purely in euphemism."

I led us all to a hotel I knew was just a block away. I'd of course never been in it, but I assumed it would be fine. It wasn't. It was what is quaintly known as "boutique." Which, in Manhattan, means "tiny shithole." The hotel's lobby saw a front desk clerk sleeping behind bulletproof glass. I figured we would have to lobby the girls to stay, but, amazingly, they didn't flinch. Even after Les paid the front desk guy in cash.

The rickety elevator took us to a room small as a janitor's closet with nothing more than a cracked mirror, a rabbit ears TV, and nothing even remotely resembling a minibar.

"It's nice." Beatrice tried to put on a happy face. "But, where's the…bed?"

We all looked around before I reached toward the ceiling, grabbed a string with a hook on the end of it, and pulled. A Murphy bed crashed to the carpet, dust flying into the air, illuminated by the full moon outside.

The four of us stared at each other dumbfounded. "What the fuck do we do now?" looks stained our pusses. I'm sure the women's pussies would have had similar looks. "Get us the fuck out of here before you make us fuck them!" they were surely shouting through their Victoria's Secret masks.

"So...are you guys...sharing this bed?"

Les and I looked at each other.

"Well..."

"We are brothers."

It was nearing 5:00 AM and our options were limited. Followers need leaders, so I had no other choice. From my pocket I pulled my green card from the restaurant, held it up toward Tinsley, and ordered her: "Go to the bathroom, strip naked, and I'll be in there in a sec."

She wordlessly did as she was told, though I thought I heard her pussy yelling out, like a man falling down a well, as she entered the bathroom and closed the door behind her.

"I love you, brother."

I gave Les a hug. Bea stood stunned by my act of prestidigitation. Just as she was about to speak up, I held the red card in her face.

"You of all people should be happy she's about to meet my meat. It'll be a great adventure for us both."

I entered the bathroom to find Tinsley naked and standing in the tub. We began ravenously making out, me holding up the green card any time I wanted her to go further in this strangest sex game ever.

Just a few hours later, the four of us awoke in that tiny Murphy bed. I didn't want to know what happened on the 75% of bedspace beside me. At least I had Tinsley as a buffer, like those bumpers you throw up to help uncoordinated kids bowl better.

Les's big meeting was in just thirty minutes. As he scrambled to get dressed, I tried to shake the women awake. I've always been amazed how deeply somnolent one-night stands can be. I didn't need any help from the green card as I screamed:

"Let's gooooooooooooooooooooo!!!!!!"

Soon outside, Johnny and I stood facing these two beautiful women, unable to break the morning-after ice. I finally spoke up, addressing the elephant in the room on the street.

"So how do we want to end this? Handshake? Hug? Kiss on

the cheek?"

Tinsley opted for all three.

"Will I ever see you again, Jason? Next time you visit from Chicago maybe? Or I could come visit even!"

I, of course, said yes—yes to everything—and took her number, and gave her a fake one of mine, our little tryst ending on a lie just like it had started. There was no way I could, or would, ever see her again. She would never get to know the real me. And, for the first time I realized, that really kind of sucked.

📍 **The Horse-Around Bar** (w. 55th St. & Tenth Ave.) | 2:05 AM

chapter eleven

WHY SHOULD YOU HAVE AS MUCH SEX AS HUMANLY POSSIBLE?

"I've never lied to a woman again."

"I don't believe that for a second."

I removed a business card from my wallet and handed it to Erin.

"Since then, I've always been who I was, and always said what I meant."

"Good thing lying to get a girl into bed isn't a crime. I'd certainly have been an accomplice in the past," bemoaned Cheryl.

"But the thing is, Devin, we didn't have to lie to them. They didn't care if we were brothers, or that we owned a beer gym."

"Exactly!"

"Then why did we do it? Why did you always make us do that stupid shit?"

"Because…in my head, I figured women simply couldn't like *me*. Back then I didn't think I could get girls to sleep with me by simply being who I was. I thought I always had to be someone else to succeed. The biggest lie I ever told was to myself."

"Well I didn't even sleep with Beatrice. We just talked all night."

I didn't even want to know about what.

We had moved to The Horse-Around, a tiny beer bar with a great tap selection. Sam, a friend of mine, was bartending. He leaned into our group, smiling toward the women. "Isn't it funny how, when drinking at a bar, men love recounting *other* nights they were drinking at a bar? Do they know nothing else of this world?" He winked at Erin and walked off to fulfill another order at the slowly-emptying-out bar.

"Prick." I was joking.

Erin smiled across the bar at him.

"Would those girls have wanted to fuck plain ol' me and plain ol' Les? Perhaps. Maybe if we'd been as equally as charming as the Stanton brothers. But we never even gave them that opportunity. And that was unfair to both of us. So for that I'm sorry, Les."

"It's a great disqualifier right from the get-go. You lie and tell a woman you like opera, just to impress her, and now you're spending every Sunday at Lincoln Center as opposed to watching football." Cheryl smiled. "Though, for the record, I fucking hate opera."

"Then I think I fucking love you, Cheryl," I added.

"But, Devin, oh wise *wise* Devin, aren't you worried about not being able to attract women now? Due to such blunt honesty where you quickly reveal yourself as a perverted asshole?" Erin smiled. "And, yes, I am trying to block your cock from my sweet, sweet friend."

"Well, it sounds like she's already taken any way."

Cheryl solemnly nodded at me.

"*Good.*"

"Erin, my behavior just eliminates the Paradox of Choice. With tons less women interested in a relationship with a perverted asshole like me, I have less choice for women I can even pursue." I took a sip of my beer. "Shit, for all we know, there might truly only be one woman on planet earth who could even put up with me!"

"Hopefully one less than that," Erin snarked.

Cheryl leaned in. "Despite what Erin says, even she realizes honesty is the most important value with us women. She just doesn't like the ugly truth and thinks she'd prefer a beautiful lie. But I know you all have sordid pasts. Some more sordid than others, but *all* of them fucking disgusting."

"Only people that fear something lie. My past is my past. If a woman cares about my past then she's mad at me for acting twenty-two years old when I was twenty-two years old. And that's just dumb."

"We all have to make mistakes when we're young. Unfortunately, or hilariously, most of them are going to be sexual," Cheryl added.

"Earlier tonight Les was whining to me that kids in school should be taught 'Don't have sex.'" Les's face began to redden. "I bit my tongue, bud, but man, I wanted to knock you off your barstool. What a stupid thing to say! Sex got us to this point."

"Great," droned Erin. "No more monologues please…"

I ignored her.

"Cavemen wandered the savannah hunting food. Then one caveman got good at hurling rocks at cougars—the animal, not like, hot old ladies. He was the world's first sports superstar and cavewomen took notice. He was now also eating better than other cavemen and looking healthier too. Thus, the cavewomen couldn't control themselves and had to have sex with him.

"Now the other sexless cavemen were forced to take notice. They too had to hone the skill of throwing rocks. Some cavemen had equal skills and would likewise impress women and pass on their genes. The other inferior cavemen and their inferior genes would soon die out.

"In future generations, *every* caveman would be able to throw rocks well. That would no longer impress cave chicks and get you laid. So what to do? Perhaps, one caveman starting painting cave walls. Again, the cavewomen took notice at this caveman so good at hunting that he had plenty of leisure time to do a seemingly worthless task like painting walls. Now every cavewoman wanted to have sex with this creative genius. And soon, sick of masturbating while staring at cave paintings of nude bush women and their bushes, other cavemen would have to show they too could exhibit these same skills if they too ever wanted to get laid again.

"On and on, each new generation exhibiting more advanced skills than the previous. Why? To impress women. An arms race simply to get into women's loincloths. Those men that were unable to keep up, watched their genes die out in a pair of paleolithic gym socks. Those men who could, not only helped advance the human race, but got tons and tons of prehistoric pussy."

Cheryl laughed hard, nearly choking on her beer.

"And, just like that, here we all sit." I raised my beer glass. "Let's toast all those cavemen and cavewomen all the way up to our parents who never said: 'Fuck sex.'" Cheryl enthusiastically clinked glasses with me. "That's what I think they should teach in schools, Les."

"Jesus, I'd love to hear you speak to a sixth grade class."

"So would I!" I stood up. "I'd tell 'em: 'Smart people get the most sex!' That'd get their attention.

"*You think it's cool to be dumb? It's not. You think girls will want to fuck you when you're older if you're dumb? They won't.* I'd tell 'em girls like guys who are clever and original. And rich. *You get all those ways by being…smart.*

"*You think of something funny to say to her—because you're smart.*

"*You think of something witty to do—because you're smart.*

"*You make money, earn respect, gain power—because you're smart.*

"You get to have sex with a woman…"

I looked at Les and Cheryl, trying to prompt them but they didn't follow.

"'*BECAUSE. YOU'RE. SMART!!!*'"

I sat back down.

"You see, I'd make being smart cool. And having lots of sex even cooler."

Aaron Goldfarb | 139

"Maybe everyone isn't as obsessed with sex as you are?" Erin offered. "Maybe some kids want to learn math and stuff."

"I'm not obsessed."

"Yeah, right."

"Well, I'm not anymore."

"'Not anymore?!' Devin, you've spent this entire bar crawl talking about sex!"

Cheryl and Erin nodded in agreement as they looked at me.

"In fact, you talk about sex more than any person I've *ever* met—and that's saying something considering the creeps in this town."

"What do they say, a guy thinks about sex every eight seconds? No surprise, Devin, you've managed to get that time down to every two or three seconds!" Cheryl laughed.

"I may talk about it a lot, but it no longer dominates my thoughts. Actually, the last half-year has been the most productive of my entire life."

Les finally examined my business card laying in the middle of the bar.

DEVIN SATYR

Google Me

"Les, all the problems in *your* life can be boiled down to one simply fact."

"Oh yeah? What's that?"

"You haven't fucked enough."

I took my business card from Les's hands and flipped it to the other side. It was as bright green as one of those churrascaria cards.

"But, I finally have."

lesson number eight

"TO DO" IS MORE IMPORTANT THAN "I DO"

I remember it was a scorching hot July day that would have been better spent at the ballpark. Jenn, Les, and I sat in that order in a pew at St. John's church, a real toilet bowl. Tripp and Tori—old high school friends of ours, old high school sweethearts to each other—were the bride and groom at this boring wedding. They stood flanked by their parents and respective wedding parties, college and "real life" friends of theirs who had replaced their high school friends like us in their lives in both importance, prominence, and desire to have them standing on the altar in ascending height.

The priest, John, or maybe Thomas, stood between Tripp and Tori. He was a nervous fellow, not speaking with any conviction, which has to be scary if you truly wanted to believe his bullshit.

"Today we gather for the wedding of, uh, Tripp Towson and Tori Hamilton, a union which defines 'love' (that's definition #2 on Dictionary.com) in its truest form..."

I whispered to Les, "Tori's mom is pretty hot, huh?" nodding toward the altar.

Les whispered back into my ear, "Mrs. Hamilton's like sixty! And married."

"'Mizzzzzzz." I snapped off the z like a slithering snake.

Aaron Goldfarb | 141

"Mizzzz Hamilton is separated from her husband. And she's sixty-two, I've just found out."

"OK…"

"You know what that means?"

Les grabbed a bible from the pew-back and held it in front of my face like I was Dracula.

"*Victoria. From the day I met you in eighth grade, I knew you were 'The One' for me…*" Up front, Tripp pulled out an index card on which he'd written his vows. Nothing says you truly meant something like an inability to memorize it. "*My best friend and eternal life partner. I promise to love you forever. Through thick or through thin…*"

I moved the bible away from my face, whispering some more to Les.

"Tori's looking thin, huh? But you know she'll soon be thick again. Especially after that Spanish honeymoon. Those tapas will make her ass far less tappable."

"*Whether we ultimately become upper-upper class, or simply remain middle-upper class…*"

I couldn't believe what I was hearing.

"If they're going to write their own vows, they should at least be realistic!"

"Shhhhhh."

"Here's what they should say…"

And, from then on, when either Tripp or Tori spoke, I whispered loudly into Les's ear what I thought their vows *should* have been.

"'…and Victoria, my love, I promise to eventually get sick of you. To one day be repulsed by your sagging tits and wrinkly skin, your annoying habits, and your stupid fucking friends.'"

I imagined Tori's stupid fucking friends feigning shock.

"'….ultimately, I promise to resent you. To hate my marriage—my life!—forcing me to act out and cheat with a hot twenty-five-year-old on a business trip seven years from now.'"

That seven-year itch was going to be scratched on the underside of some Chili's bartender's g-spot in an Avis rental car in a Howard Johnson parking lot near the San Antonio airport.

Tripp grabbed both of Tori's hands.

"'…I will one day *loathe* you.'"

"*…through sickness and through health, 'til death do us part.*"

The priest nodded at Tori that it was her turn.

"*Tripp. My handsome man. My new husband…*"

"'I promise to never give you a blowjob again. To immediately begin complaining about our living conditions, until you purchase an 8000-square-foot house in Westchester. A beach house on Shelter Island. A new Lex for me…'"

Les scrunched up his face, trying to concentrate on the ceremony.

"'I will force you to get me pregnant within the next six months. Not because I like kids, but so my lazy ass never has to work again and I can commit to a life of clothes shopping and stroller-pushing and "Tasti D" licking with my annoying fucking friends.'"

I imagined her annoying fucking friends feigning shock yet again.

"'Finally, my darling, I promise to quit getting my vagina waxed. I'm married now, and that would be *gauche*.'"

They clenched hands and, pleased with myself, I finally quit whispering.

"*I, Victoria Hamilton, wish to be your wife!*"

They finished their vows and said "*I do*" and kissed and the audience cheered and my brain booed.

As Tripp and Tori wedding-marched out of the church to that one song, Ms. Hamilton turned to watch her daughter and new son-in-law's exit. I saw my chance and made strong eye contact with her. I was the only person in the entire room not looking at the bride and groom at that second in time.

Four hours in time, five scotches for me, and six champagnes for her later, I completed my vow to myself and Ms. Hamilton and I were lying in room 514's bed, post-coitus. You might care to know the pre-coital details that got me from church to her suite, thinking those are what is truly pertinent in this guide for a single man. But those details are surprisingly irrelevant. Nothing special, nothing lucky, nothing sober. Any man—any persistent and clever man—coulda done it. Persistence is pertinent here.

"Menopause rules." I raised my arms in exultation.

"Got that right, sweetheart. Rubbers are now obsolete."

"I don't think we'll ever see a public service message that says that."

Ms. Hamilton lit up a cigarette.

"And I love that you actually smoke after sex. No one from my generation smokes in bed after sex. I feel like I'm in an old James Bond movie."

"Did you enjoy my pussy galore?"

Ms. Hamilton barely paid attention to me as she said that. I didn't care as I continued paying attention to her bareness. She had a surprisingly great body.

"Is this weird for you, Mizzzz Hamilton?"

She stared at me, knowing I was trying to ruffle her feathers.

"Devin, you were by far the cutest single man at this wedding."

"That's nice to hear."

"Don't get too cocky. Your competition was the Seniors Tour. Lee Trevino, Chi Chi Rodriguez, and Fuzzy fuckin' Zoeller."

"Ouch."

"You would have thought my daughter and son-in-law could have sprung for some sexy gigolos to pretend they were wedding guests."

"What a novel idea! I'll make sure to hire some when I get married."

"Don't. Unless you're sure. You know the stats?"

"50% failure rate?"

Ms. Hamilton nodded. "And how many of those 50% who 'succeed' are miserable?"

"At least people no longer stay together out of obligation.

I actually like seeing an increasing divorce rate. Means people who have gone down the wrong fork in the road are now having no issue in turning back and heading down a new one."

"Most people are only into marriage for the forks any way. And the China, Dutch ovens, wine racks…"

"Oh shit! I forgot to get a gift for them."

"Don't bother. You came."

"I certainly did."

"Devin, more marriages 'worked' back in the day because of the divorce stigma. People were even less happy in the days when they couldn't get divorced. A divorced person can be unhappy. A person that wants to get divorced but can't, is goddamn miserable."

"Seems like marriages fail because people are more concerned with the one-day wedding than the next fifty years of *weddedness*."

"I'm afraid that may be true with my daughter."

I lied through my teeth. "Oh, I'm sure it's not. Their vows seemed…*credible*."

"I hope they have no regrets. I spent my entire marriage full of regret. You know, I didn't have my first one-night stand 'til I was fifty-nine. Met my ex-husband at eighteen and he was my only lover from then until we separated three years back."

"Interesting."

"Sex is a lot easier now. And I've got a helluva lot of catching up to do."

"That's beautiful to hear."

"Sex used to be such a big thing. Especially for two people of my generation. All you young kids have been fucking freely since grade school though. Right?"

"Well…"

Ms. Hamilton walked over to the minibar and prepared something using the tiny bottles available. I leaned over the bed to my suit pants lying on the floor and grabbed for my wallet.

"Cheers."

She handed me a vodka soda.

"Indeed. This did call for a little celebration."

"Well it wasn't that big of deal. It was just sex."

"Oh, it was big for me."

I pulled a wrinkled piece of paper out of my wallet. It had been there for over a decade.

"What's that?"

"I assume you're mature enough to handle it."

"I can handle whatever ya got. I was born in the '40s you know."

"I know."

I passed the paper to her and she studied it curiously.

"'*RedheadTwinsSouthAmericanMileHighPublic1980s*…?'"

"It's…"

"What's this….box next to…1940s?"

"The *only* unchecked box I have left."

I paused.

"It's my…sexual to-do list."

Ms. Hamilton perused the paper a bit more, then looked at me, having an "Aha!" about her hoohah.

"I…"

She slowly put two and two together. I was glad she'd quickly pulled her two legs apart.

"I…"

As she stood over me in my bed, a weird look on her face, I was now worried she was hurt. That was the last thing I wanted.

"I just figured from an early age I should pursue everything, try things out, so I had no regrets, like you said, by the time I was finally ready to settle down. I figured it would eventually lead to a 100% happy marriage with my final partner."

"And tonight you checked off my old lady box, huh?!"

Ms. Hamilton grabbed her purse on the nightstand and reached for some tissues.

"No, no, it's not like that. I swear. You're a beautiful woman, Vivian, and I've had a great time. I wasn't *just* doing this because of some silly…"

From her fancy cigarette case, Ms. Hamilton pulled out a

piece of paper.

"1978?" She raised her eyebrows.

"What?"

"I said: 1978?!"

"Yes, that's right."

The paper she handed me was typewritten on high-bond stationary with "VLH" at the top.

"Well great then."

I scanned her list.

"Why don't *you* check the appropriate box, darling."

DS's
Sexual Checklist

- ☒ White
- ☒ Black
- ☐ Latino
- ☐ Asian
- ☒ Indian
- ☐ Native Americ.
- ☒ over 6'
- ☒ under 5'
- ☒ over 200lbs?
- ☒ Genius
- ☒ 1990s
- ☒ Born 1980s
- ☒ Born 70s
- ☒ Born 60s
- ☒ Born 50s
- ☒ (Born 40s!)

- ☒ MARRIED/engaged
- ☒ DIVORCED
- ☒ TWINS ☒ Apart
- ☒ 3some ☒ together

- ☒ Shower
- ☒ BUTT
- ☒ CAR
- ☒ Moving Car
- ☒ BOAT
- ☒ SPM =

- ☐ Virgin
- ☒ Total Slut
- ~~Tranie?~~
- ☒ Dr.
- ☒ Cop
- ☒ Prof./teacher
- ☒ parents'
- ☒ Friend
- ☒ Mile High
- ☒ Celebrity
- ☒ w/in hour of meeting

- ☒ Blonde
- ☒ Brown
- ☒ Red Head
- ☒ Europe
- ☒ Asia
- ☒ S. Amer.
- ☒ STRIPPER
- ☒ Deaf
- ☒ Porn Actress

- ~~Gay?~~
- ☒ School
- ☒ Hospital
- ☒ Porn-like?
- ☒ Aus.
- ☒ Antarctica
- ☒ (anal)
- ☒ Super $$$
- ☒ Actress on stage

♥ **Mario's Big Pie** (54th & Ninth Ave.) | 2:35 AM

chapter twelve
WHY DO YOU NEED TO SEXUALLY GRADUATE?

"What kind of creeper would make a list like that?!"

Erin scanned the yellowing piece of notebook paper I'd removed from my wallet.

"It's good to have goals, Erin."

Les carefully examined it, a hint of accusation in his slightly slurred voice.

"When did you make this thing?"

We were now eating pizza slices nearly as big as stadium pennants, as was Mario's gimmick. They were our gut sponges, needed to mop up hours of alcohol.

"Just after I'd lost my virginity to another middle-class, white, public-school-educated, sixteen-year-old virgin." I looked at Cheryl, explaining. "It had been predictably awful."

She nodded in feigned empathy.

"After that experience, I knew I needed to know more things. In fact, I was obsessed with how little I knew. Instead of being thrilled with popping my cherry, I spent all night fretting about the cherries I still didn't know about. About the things I might want to know in my sexual life before I'd be ready to ever possibly have a married life."

"So...? *Are* you ready?" Cheryl wondered.

"I think I am. If a certain woman is ever willing."

"That's just a line, Cher," Erin said.

"I assure you it isn't."

I took my sexual checklist and put it to the flame of a tiny votive candle sitting next to the crushed red pepper and Parmesan cheese shakers.

"I accomplished it all," I proudly noted.

"Well don't you deserve a diploma," Les snarked.

"No, I deserve to speak at a college commencement."

* * *

Trustees, faculty, family, friends, and, most importantly, graduates...I am honored to speak to you on this momentous occasion.

I could talk about how this university is more than simply a step between high school and the real world. It's a stepping stone to your futures.

I could preach the importance that this not be the end of your educations, but the start.

But that's all bullshit. All that matters as you enter the real world is this:

Have as much sex as possible!

As quickly as possible!

So you can get on with your fucking lives.

So you can start making good decisions.

Ones not based on sex.

When I was at this university, there could have been a foot of snow on the ground, I could have had the flu, an important final exam at 7 AM, and have just jerked off (though the internet was still dial-up back then)...but if I got a phone call at 4 AM from the ugliest girl on campus, one who lived halfway across campus, begging me to come "hang out"—I would.

Now?

Now, I might not even leave the house during rush house on a slightly breezy day if Giselle told me she'd just dumped Tom Brady because of me and had a limo outside waiting to whisk me to her.

And you know why that is? Because I've finally had enough sex that it no longer dominates my thoughts. It no longer leads to me making bad decisions and doing things I don't want to do. My mind is now sharp, because my dick is no longer constantly hard.

Female graduates, I see you looking confused, "Does this apply to us?!" Absolutely. You will never be as promiscuous as the horndogs you're graduating with hope to be, but sex still predominates your thoughts and leads to you making bad decisions.

Bad decisions about love.

I would encourage you women to quickly learn how frivolous sex can be to a guy. Just because he walks through a foot of snow at 4 AM to come "hang out," doesn't mean he loves you. Men are despicable. Know that. Embrace that.

OK, sure, you male graduates are now applauding me for essentially encouraging the women to slut it up more, but it's true. It's a benefit to both sexes to put less weight on sex.

Because, you see, ultimately, you will know when the sex you're having is important.

But until then, get it out of your system.
Stay safe.
Stay focused.
Fuck often, and conquer.

* * *

Cheryl mockingly applauded me with a golf clap. Les and Erin remained staring at me after my mock speech.

"Stephanie Mitchell!"

"Huh?"

He was clearly drunk and becoming surly.

"I said: 'Stephanie Mitchell.'"

"Who?"

The sexual checklist had burned to black embers on the

empty pizza tray in front of us, an unpleasant smell rising from the center of the table.

"Stephanie fucking Mitchell."

"What about her?

"Who is Stephanie Mitchell?" Cheryl wondered.

"'*Who* is Stephanie Mitchell?' Why don't you tell her about Stephanie Mitchell, Devin?"

"Why would I?"

"You like to tell stories. Sex stories. Sexy sex stories to impress every one. You claim you're not ashamed to tell these two girls of your past. So why don't you tell them both about Stephanie Mitchell."

Cheryl and Erin were now intrigued as to who/what/why Stephanie Mitchell was.

"Uh, I believe Stephanie…went to high school with Les and me." The night had quickly become uncomfortable and it was only going to get worse. "I haven't thought of that name in a long time, bud."

"What else is Stephanie Mitchell?"

"Stephanie Mitchell is…"

"Stephanie Mitchell *is*…what'd you just call her? The 'middle-class, white, public school virgin' *who* Devin lost his virginity to."

"I, uh…"

"Devin, you said a women shouldn't be mad at you for acting like a twenty-two-year-old when you were twenty-two."

"Yes…"

"But what about you acting like a sixteen-year-old when you were sixteen?"

"I'm still not sure what…?"

"I loved Stephanie Mitchell…"

It all came rushing back to me. Les had been obsessed with Stephanie Mitchell since junior high. He'd pathetically fawned over her with no clue how to possibly date her, until one day, out of the blue, she asked him to our school's Christmas Dance. At the dance, he was too nervous to ask Stephanie to dance, so he didn't. He was too nervous to pull her into a corner of the gymnasium and steal a kiss, so he didn't.

"The whole time at that dance I was wondering what I was supposed to be doing. A haunting voice in my head kept saying 'Kiss her, Les, kiss her, kiss her.' But I never did. And I had to be home by midnight to beat curfew."

"You should have just blown the curfew off."

"Like you? *You* didn't have a curfew, Devin. And, neither did Stephanie. In fact, your dad let you have kids over for an after-dance beer blast. Including Stephanie."

Erin groaned, now knowing where this was headed.

"I guess that night you made this stupid checklist, huh?"

Les dropped his half-finished slice atop the ashes.

"Is that when you checked box number one: 'fuck best friend's girlfriend'?"

Les looked me firmly in the eyes, now unable to speak. I tried to defend myself, but just dug a deeper hole.

"But…Stephanie only liked you…as a *friend*. As you just said, you'd never even kissed."

"How was I supposed to know?"

Les stood up.

"You weren't. We were just stupid sixteen-year-olds."

He pounded his hand on the table.

"No! I was a stupid sixteen-year-old. And you were fucking stupid sixteen-year-olds!"

I put my hands on Les's shoulders, trying to ease him back into the booth.

"Why have you never said anything about this before, bud?"

I could feel Cheryl and Erin staring at us.

"What could I say? That because I was a clueless pussy, you swooped in for the pussy?"

"I was horny and impetuous."

"That's the Satyr you are. Even stealing my girl."

I felt for him, but I'd had enough of his inaccurate whining.

"No one's girl!!! Not then. And certainly not now."

Les headed for the door, charging out of the pizzeria as I

Aaron Goldfarb | 153

called after him.

"Stupid Stephanie is a mother of three now! Look her up on Facebook and get the fuck over it!"

But he was already out the door. Erin and Cheryl glared at me, both clearly somewhat disgusted, but only Erin spoke.

"Just like I said: you're an asshole."

She got up, grabbed Les's dump box, and ran out the door after him. I looked at Cheryl.

"You know, I never thought I was."

"What?"

"I guess I really am an asshole like everyone says."

Cheryl gently put her hands on top of mine.

"Based on what you've shown me, I really don't think you are."

"Well…that's nice to hear."

"Come on, let's go find your friend."

📍 **Flaming Saddles** (53rd and Ninth Ave.) | 2:45 AM

chapter thirteen

WHY DOES FORTUNE FAVOR THE BOLD...OR AT LEAST ASSURE HE GETS LAID?

Cheryl and I eventually walked outside to find Erin a few storefronts down, standing outside a bar called Flaming Saddles.

"He went in there."

"Uh, this is a gay bar." If the small rainbow decal on the front door didn't give that away, the beefy bear in a sleeveless vest checking IDs surely did.

"I know, genius."

"Hmmm. So, I guess he has finally decided to say: 'Fuck sex.'"

"Or he's opting for a new kind of it."

"No," Erin explained, "He just said he was sick of being around men and women hitting on each other."

We looked at Erin.

"Does that exclude you, hon?"

"Hey, I told him *to* hit on me."

"And, what did he say to that?"

"He said, 'I *can't*.'"

"And…?"

"I said, 'You *can*. You just have to start talking.'"

I smiled. "I told him the same thing."

Erin shrugged and the three of us entered the western-themed saloon. It was packed to the gills with men sipping longnecks, line dancing, and riding a pink mechanical bull. Garth Brooks's "Friends in Low Places" played. I overheard one guy crack to a friend, "I only have friends if they get in low places."

"*You only* have friends in *blow* places," his friend corrected.

Erin and Cheryl headed off in one direction while I walked through the crowd looking for Les. I eventually found him up at the bar talking with a bartender wearing leather chaps and a ten gallon hat. And that was it.

"Hey, bud."

Les turned toward me but didn't respond.

"Look, I'm sorry."

"I don't want to talk to you."

"Sounds like you don't want to talk to anybody."

"Lovers' quarrel?" wondered the gaytender.

Les scoffed at him.

"Hardly."

Les sounded pretty gay saying that, and the gaytender mocked him. "Haaaardly."

"We are fighting, but we're not gay." Les further explained.

"You're seriously still mad I fucked your high school girlfriend?"

"And you think we're the pervs," said the gaytender.

"In *high school*," I added.

"Because that was it. The one point in time that changed both our lives."

"Get real."

"I am real. That's the point that instantly set you up for this charmed life you now lead. While *not* fucking Stephanie really fucked me up. Reverse things and maybe we're different people by now."

"Yeah, well, we certainly wouldn't be sitting at this gay rodeo bar."

The bartender brought us two shots of something neon green, noting, "For the *not*-lovers." He snickered.

"Look, Les, I'll only say it one more time: I'm truly sorry for fucking Stephanie Whatever-her-name-is-now."

He threw back the shot.

"Oliver. Her married name is Oliver."

I couldn't help but laughing.

"What?!"

I threw back my shot. Not bad.

"I'm laughing because I *know*. I've looked her up too."

Les couldn't help himself from slightly smiling.

"Her Facebook life looks really fucking boring. Was she always so religious?"

"Yeah. She was. And it's not funny. You hurt me and…I guess I've been harboring a grudge all this time."

"Hey bud, it's not like fucking Stephanie set me on any great path in life. No matter what you think."

We glanced over to the dance floor where Erin and Cheryl were now drunkenly line-dancing. They were clueless, but cute.

"You straight guys just don't get it."

We turned back to the gaytender, who had clearly been listening in.

"What?"

"You guys just don't understand how to exist as single men. It's really pathetic to watch. Hilariously pathetic to watch."

"And you do?"

"What? Gay guys can be single guys too. I mean, it's cutthroat out there as a single gay. Look around."

We did. The testosterone in the air was thick with buff dudes. It was somehow emasculating me.

"Yeah, but you lucky assholes don't have to deal with women."

"So…?"

"If I was a single gay my dick would have fallen off by now."

"It's not that easy. Gay guys can't just sit back and hope the world unfolds in front of them."

"I bet if they're buff and have a giant cock they can."

"OK, maybe. But for the rest of us, remember: *Audentes fortuna juvat.*"

I had no clue what he was saying, but nerdy Les did, of

course.

"'Fortune favors the bold.'"

"Very good!" The man look impressed with Les, lightly giving him a love tap on his cheek. That seemed to quickly sober Les up.

"May I tell you a story about me and my best friend?"

"Why the hell not?" Les shrugged. "Everyone else has told a story tonight."

* * *

I was back home in my Nebraska cow town at the closest thing we had to a country club.

A sign above the dais read "Welcome Putnam Valley Class of 1998!"

At the dais, Courtney Long, our former class Vice President, stood behind the lectern, boring the entire room.

"...and I'll be brief with a summary of senior year..."

I had hated every second of that year. So I didn't need a fucking recap.

I sat at a table with my female friend Jamie and seven other reuniters.

"I should have never come back to Omaha," I lamented.

"Huh? What'd you say?" Jamie was still ignoring me, her eyes locked on the front of the room. On another member of the reunion dais, Rick Hooper.

"Our high school reunion? How gay is this?!"

"Don't say that."

"I'm allowed to call something gay. This speech is just so *so* gay."

But she still wouldn't even make eye contact with me, wouldn't unlock those eyes from Rick.

"Great. I don't have a date to bring so I have to be a fag to my hag."

That line finally got Jamie to turn. No one likes to be called a hag. Especially by a fag like me.

"Watch it."

"I knew I shouldn't come. We should be back in New York and I should be doing gay things with gay men."

"You can't pass up free booze, Bradlee."

"You got me there."

I toasted the sentiment and threw back a watery Manhattan. My "free booze." Only a $480 round-trip plane ticket, three nights of staying in my parents' basement, where I still lived in the closet, and totally being ignored at dinner by my so-called best friend.

"Look at Rick Hooper up there. You know I've had a crush on him since sixth grade."

At this point I figured, if my friend was going to marginalize me, I would have to maximize that marginalization.

"You should go after him, girlfriend." I sassed it up like I was the poofy, swishy, lispy sidekick to the female lead in a romantic comedy.

"Should I?"

And, for the first time, Jamie actually seemed interested in what I had to say. Only because I was saying it about her and reinforcing her desires.

"Absolutely, sister. You look absolutely *fab-solutely* hot as shit, bitch!"

Sometimes, I liked making myself a stereotype, especially outside of New York where folks had less subtle gaydar.

Jamie smoothed her dress.

"You think he'll remember me?"

"No. But that's a good thing, sisterfriend. You've reinvented yourself. You're the prettiest girl here now."

"You're right!" She turned toward me. "I'm totally going to make out with Rick tonight."

Jamie, her eyes still on Rick, grabbed my hand.

"You have to come with me for support though."

"Of course! It's what I'm here for, you big slut."

Gay guys like me could totally say misogynistic things and heterosexual women never seemed to care.

Aaron Goldfarb | 159

Jamie scooted toward Rick, dragging me a foot behind her like some gay Radio Flyer.

"Great speech!"

Rick turned and smiled at us.

"Hey!

Rick searched his memory bank. But, the bank seemed to be closed for the weekend.

"Jamie, right?"

Rick peeked over her shoulder and eyed me.

"And Bradlee!"

I was quite surprised he even knew my name.

"Yes, that's right."

Jamie butted back in.

"I never thought you'd remember me."

"I could never forget you two. The dynamic duo! You guys went to the prom together, right?"

He smiled at Jamie, who now looked embarrassed.

"I was sooooo jealous."

Now Jamie swooned. But I rolled my eyes so much I was surprised they didn't get a good look at my brain. Rick leaned in toward us.

"Hey, wanna join me outside for a smoke?"

Soon, the three of us were standing around a putting green passing a joint around.

"...and then I moved to New York and had a few boyfriends but I never forgot you..."

Rick clearly looked uncomfortable with all of Jamie's gushing. I was bored to tears though. I wished she was, like, famous enough to have a Wikipedia page so Rick could quickly read that instead of listening to her detail her whole boring bio.

"...I always felt that, though we never spoke once in high school..."

Rick struggled to get a word in edgewise.

"...we had some sort of karmic connection."

Jamie smiled. Rick smiled. Rick slowly grabbed Jamie's hand and brought it toward him.

Jamie turned and looked at me. For the first time all night our eyes met. She raised those eyebrows above those fucking eyes and mouthed to me: "Leave!"

Jamie turned back to Rick.

"So tell me what've you been up to these last ten years…"

Oh, I was seething! I just had to lean in and interrupt her.

"Actually, before I leave…?"

I stepped in front of Jamie so her grip on Rick broke.

"I'm surprised you knew my name, Rick, because I think most people in high school merely knew me as the quiet kid who was clearly gay but refused to admit he was. They were right. For my whole life I've taken a backseat to my desires, followed others' path for me, and been nothing more than her sidekick. Some comic relief. The supporting character of my own life."

Some trapped pot smoke released from my lungs. Fortune favors the bold who are emboldened by pot.

"Well, I'm tired of it. Earlier tonight, Jamie was telling me all about how she had a crush on you in high school. Well guess what? I did too."

Rick swallowed and I had no choice but to backtrack, quickly trying to speak my way out of the awkwardness, and possibly a punch from the ex-football player.

"I just wanted to tell you that, Rick, before I go back inside to leave you two alone to make out or whatever you're gonna do tonight."

I had said my bold piece, yet I was already cursing my boldness as I turned to walk away. Rick reached out and grabbed the back of my blazer.

"Don't."

I spun around.

"When I said earlier I was jealous you two went to the prom together…I didn't mean I was jealous of *you*."

I was shocked. Then I got it. I turned to Jamie and raised *my* eyebrows, mouthing:

"LEAVE!"

Aaron Goldfarb | 161

* * *

"BULLSHIT!"

"I swear."

I looked at Les.

"So you see? I'm not the *worst* best friend in the world."

Just then a man came over and kissed Bradlee on the lips.

"Ew, smoky breath."

"Hi, Ricky, hon. I was just telling my new friends about the day I finally decided to carve my own path in life."

Rick looked at us curiously and smiled.

"I like when he starts carving paths."

That was clearly a gay entendre, but I didn't get it. In the corner Erin and Cheryl danced to "Cotton-Eyed Joe" as gay guys surrounded them applauding.

Bradlee put his arm around Rick and smiled at us.

"Remember Les: pussies don't get pussy. Now call that girl over here and let's have another drink on the house."

♀ Flaming Saddles (53rd and Ninth Ave.) | 3:05 AM

chapter fourteen

SHOULD YOU SEND YOUR KIDS TO THE MACHIAVELLI SCHOOL FOR CHILDREN?

We lifted the ski to our faces and chugged. The "shot-ski" had four shot glasses attached to it, forcing everyone to do a shot of cheap vodka at the exact same time.

"So where should we end the night?" Les asked.

"You've finally decided you're happy to be out?"

"It's 3 AM. There's really no time to make other plans now is there?"

I laughed.

"Another bar? I'm ready to get in bed, Cher."

"C'mon, one more." Cheryl put her arm around Erin.

"Fine."

"Great. Let's go back to where we started. Drunx."

"You guys started there?" Erin looked surprised. "We were there too! What time? We must have just missed each other!"

We headed north on Tenth Avenue, Cheryl and Erin walking a few feet ahead of us, whispering about girl stuff.

"You know…that Stephanie Mitchell thing makes me finally realize my biggest problem. The problem no guide can overcome."

"What's that?"

Aaron Goldfarb

"My parents raised me the wrong way."
"Your parents are awesome."
"That's the problem."
"How so?"
"My parents raised me to be a nice person."
"What's wrong with that?"
"Nothing really, oh, except the fact it's never helped me in getting the most important thing in the world."

Cheryl and Erin looked back, smiling curiously based on whatever they had been whispering about.

"At the start of the night you were 'Fuck sex,' and now it's back to the most important thing in the world?"

"At the start of the night I was dumped and sober. Now I'm drunk and have a hot girl's ass in my sights."

I looked ahead of us. Erin did indeed have a nice ass.

"Getting laid isn't the most important thing in life, Les."
"Then what is?"
"Love."

Les drunkenly cackled in my face.

"Good one."
"I'm being serious, bud."
"I know you are. But it sure took you getting laid a ton to determine that. Wouldn't we all like such a body of research."
"Then build one."
"It's too late for me."
"It's never too late."
"It is, don't worry about it." Les smiled. "But wait 'til you see how I raise *my* children. I'll give them all the opportunities I never had! Shit, maybe I'll start an institution even!"
"A what?"
"I can envision the infomercial…

"MACHIAVELLI SCHOOL FOR CHILDREN"
SHOOTING SCRIPT

FADE IN:

EXT. MACHIAVELLI SCHOOL FOR CHILDREN - DAY

It would take place on palatial facility that looks like a college campus.

An older (60 or so) ME walks onto screen. I'm of course speaking in an amped-up pitchman mode.

          DR. LES
If you're like me, your parents raised you to be Mr. Nice Guy, right? Now where are you? Home alone with your dick in your hand!

Then I'll look into the camera.

          DR. LES
Hi, I'm Dr. Lesley Mann, Founder of the Machiavelli School for Children, the only elementary learning facility that teaches children how to truly succeed once they're adults in the real world.

INT. CLASSROOM - DAY

We'd now see a six-year-old boy approach a six-year-old girl. I go on…

> DR. LES (V.O)
> Typically, boys are taught to be supplicating, worshipping, and deferential to girls.

Just like I was, right? Just like I am. So now the boy speaks to the girl.

> JOHNNY
> Hi Sadie, I'm having a birthday party this weekend. You're so pretty, I would very much like you to come.

The girl, of course, no surprise, looks REPULSED by this little wiener.

> SADIE
> Get lost, cooties creep!

Boom! An "X" appears over the screen with a buzzer sound effect. WRONG!!!

> DR. LES (V.O.)
> Now my way…the Machiavelli School for Children way!

Again, the same boy speaks to the girl.

                    JOHNNY
          Hi Sadie, I'm having a birthday
          party this weekend. You're so
          pretty, I would very much like
          you to come.
                    (a dramatic beat)
          To clean up the mess me and my
          friends are gonna make!

The boy cackles. And the girl is
crushed! She meekly responds.

                    SADIE
          OK, I'll come help if it'll make
          you happy...

And now a SMILEY FACE appears over the
screen. DING DING DING!!!"

"Are you being serious, bud?"
"Dead. But wait…there's more!…

EXT. MACHIAVELLI SCHOOL FOR CHILDREN -
DAY

Again, I talk to the camera.

                    DR. LES
          At our school, boys will be taught

such topics as...

OK, now TOPIC TITLES would stream upward on the screen, Star Wars-style. Underneath the titles, a montage of boys aged, I don't know…4 through 12 will be shown being taught such shit as:

THE FOOLISHNESS OF GIVING COMPLIMENTS
CREATING A VERISIMILITUDE OF POWER
IMPLYING YOU'RE GOOD IN BED
DETECTING "THE CRAZY" (AND AVOIDING IT)
WINGMANNING
DICTATING THINGS
THE IGNORE-HER GAME
ALOOFNESS IS VERY SEXY
MAKING GIRLS FEEL DUMB

Next, a similar MONTAGE of little girls will be shown being taught. You'll love this…

> DR. LES (V.O.)
> Don't worry females, there's classes for you too!

COCKBLOCKING
SEEING THRU HIS BULLSHIT
FLIRTING WITHOUT INTENTIONS
MAKING HIM BEG

BILKING HIM OUT OF MONEY AND THINGS
HOT & COLD BEHAVIOR
NEVER ANSWERING HIS CALLS, TEXTS, ETC.
THE FOG OF DATING
ATTENTION HOGGING
CREATING JEALOUSY

Then, in the final scene, I'll be standing behind a huge desk with a placard on it that says "DEAN." And, Devin, I smile toward the fucking camera and say proudly:

> Dr. LES
> Enroll now and I guarantee by adulthood, you won't ever feel the pain that everyone else feels in this stupid fuckin' game called love.

FADE TO BLACK.

"...So? What do you think?"

"Absurd."

"Awesome, huh?"

"Hardly. Maybe you should have Cheryl punch-up that little script."

"Huh?"

"She's a screenwriter."

"How do you know?"

"Because she told me. You know, it's good to sometimes actually ask questions to girls you want to have sex with."

But Les wasn't listening to me anymore.

"Shhhh…"

"What are you doing?!"

He had his Blackberry up to his ear, listening as the phone rang on the other end. He had a crazy look on his face.

"Are you calling Jennifer again?!"

I reached for his phone, but he jumped back like a prize-fighter avoiding a hook.

"Hello, you've reached the voicemail of Nancy Mann…"

I leaned my ear next to Les's, trying to listen in.

"What are you doing?!"

Cheryl and Erin entered Drunx, looking back toward us to see Les and me dancing ear-to-ear. I waved for them to go ahead before they saw anything even more embarrassing happen.

BEEP!

"Hi mom, this is uh…Les. Your son. You're probably sleeping right now since it's…"

Les clumsily tried to his check his watch, but couldn't focus his eyes enough to read it.

"…*late*…but, uh, I just wanted to call to thank you for raising me so well and being so nice to me and supporting me and giving me everything in life because—" I hit "END" on Les's phone before he had a chance to finish. "—it guaranteed I'm a failure as an adult!"

Les spun and angrily threw his Blackberry as far as he could.

I was surprised how strong his arm was and how aerodynamic a Blackberry was. At least they were best-in-class for something. The phone hit the third-story fire escape of a walk-up on the other side of Tenth Avenue, before tumbling to the sidewalk below and shattering into a zillion pieces.

The smoking masses in front of Drunx applauded, no doubt assuming Les was just another drunk guy pissed off by modern cellular technology and/or shitty Manhattan reception.

"What is wrong with you?!"

"Everything! Tell me my life wouldn't be better if I had been raised the Machiavellian way. Tell me that wouldn't have worked!"

"Worked how?"

"Devin, *that* was the guide I needed all along."

"No, it wasn't."

"Devin. Devin. You know I love you. But, Devin, I'd have Erin right now if I'd been raised better."

"All your school would do is create a master society of sadistic deviants."

"Correction: a master society of sadistic deviants whose parents could afford the $40,000 a year tuition."

"You don't have to be...Machiavellian to get laid. It's about making true connections."

That seemed to jar something in Les's beer-battered brain. He sprinted across the street toward the shrapnel of his phone, nearly getting hit by a stream of out-of-service taxis headed to their garage. I followed him and watched as he gathered the pieces and began trying to put the phone back together. The screen was completely shattered.

"Shit. I can't see my contact list. Give me Jenn's number."

"Why?"

"Because I had a *true connection* with her."

"You didn't."

"Fuck you. I did."

Les punched a few random numbers into his now-juryrigged phone and waited. I stood beside him, tense and anxious.

Aaron Goldfarb | 171

Surprisingly, someone picked up.

"Les?"

It was Jenn's voice. Les remained silent, unsure of what to say, looking at me for help.

"*Les? Are you OK?*"

He remained frozen.

"*This isn't funny, Les. Are you drunk?*"

Though he had become fossilized, he remained calm, a nirvana washing over him.

"*I can hear a bar in the background! Are you at that divey pit you and Devin like?*"

I held back my laughter. Les pulled the phone away from his ear and stared at it.

"*Well...THANK YOU for waking me up! You know I need my sleep on Friday nights!*"

Les looked up at me and smiled.

"*Are you ever going to say something!??!*"

Les dropped the phone in a garbage can and headed back across Tenth Avenue toward Drunx. I followed, Jenn's voice still ringing out in the distance as it sat atop a stack of Wendy's wrappers.

"*Never. Call. Me. Agaaaaaaaaaaaaaain!*"

We entered Drunx to find three random men swaying and singing along loudly to Weezer's "Say It Ain't So." We pushed past them to locate Cheryl and Erin sitting at a table by the window, a full view of the street and where we had just been. Erin smiled mischievously, she had clearly seen it all.

"Bad reception?"

"I, uh, am thinking about finally switching to the iPhone."

"Sure." Erin didn't seem to believe him, smiling coyly.

The night was winding down and the bar was emptying out, the few remaining people simply trying to make something of their evening. Or, they were all too stupid, or too drunk, to wisely cut their losses. It was mostly men, our embarrassing gender outnumbering women by about nine to one. Each man hoping that solitary one would be *their* one, like you could patiently just wait your way into a drunk girl's pants. Perhaps you could. I certainly had won that war of attrition before. Now maybe it was Les's turn with Erin. I noticed them mindlessly touching hands with each other underneath the table, just for a split second.

I hoped she would make him happy.

I hoped he had learned something tonight.

I just hoped all my work had finally taught Les the secret to life:

lesson number nine

YOU NEED TO KNOW WHAT YOU'RE LOOKING FOR

I was sitting on her couch, still in my basketball shorts and a t-shirt when she came home from work. These were the same clothes I slept in, the same clothes I spent most days in, the same clothes she'd seen me in when she'd left for work that very morning. She wasn't thrilled.

I was living in Midtown at the time, but spent most of my nights with Miriam at her Koreatown apartment. I spent most my days there too. She actually had air conditioning so I could focus better on building websites, my "job" at the time.

I'd finished for the day and was watching Pardon the Interruption while shooting at a Nerf hoop I'd placed above her door. Unfortunately, she opened the door just as I released a shot. It swished through the plastic hoop and hit her square on the crown of her head. She'd just had her hair done. The Brazilian, it was called. It straightened out women's hair and kept it that way for a few weeks. Apparently the salons used formaldehyde for the procedure. It seemed pretty dangerous but all sorts of fancy New York women were getting them done at the time. I suspected the chemicals were seeping into their brains, making them go crazy. She was certainly on that path.

"Still playing that game?!"

"Hon, it's an addiction."

"What about the neighbors?"

"No one lives below you except your hunchbacked super and some rats."

"What about beside me?"

"The Paks? They should be honored to have a living legend practicing his craft next door."

Miriam meekly walked to the kitchen where she noticed a dirty dish from lunch still in the sink. I'd made tuna salad. She clicked her tongue to the roof of her mouth. A few recently discarded beer bottles in the recycling bin made her scoff. That had been the other part of my lunch.

"Looks like you had another productive day."

"Thank you, I did. Nothing beats working for yourself. Working for the man, when you are the man. It's like masturbation. You control all the pressure and it's always satisfying."

I had been making a lot of masturbation analogies lately, which should have told me the end was near.

Miriam bit her tongue for a second before glancing at the sink again.

"Did we just decide to quit doing dishes?"

"The passive-aggressive 'we.' Nice. Very elementary school teacher."

I kept shooting at the Nerf hoop.

"At least it smells bad in here. That's something."

I slammed the Nerf ball off the floor, angrily.

"And that's the trifecta of passive aggression. Fuck! Do 'we' have something to say, Miriam?!"

Miriam was taken aback by my outburst.

"You know I hate that. Say something or don't. Passive aggression is for children."

"I'm not a...children."

"Then you must realize the things you are saying are too petty to say any way but passive aggressively."

"That's not true."

"Then say them to me! Say them to my fucking face!"

I moved closer to her.

"Say, 'Devin, how could you sit on your lazy ass all afternoon drinking beer while I work? How could you play some stupid Nerf game instead of cleaning the dishes and taking out the recycling?! Why don't you get a real job and make more money like all my friends' boyfriends?!!!' Why not just say that?! Would that be too hard? To say the truth? To say what you believe?!"

Miriam cowered. "No…"

And then it came to me. Surely the most Eureka! moment of my life.

"I just got a great idea. Let's play a game."

"What…game?"

"This game's called… 'Nothing's Too Petty To Tell Me.'"

"'Nothing's Too Petty…?'" "'…To Tell Me.'" Yes."

I adopted a booming Rod Roddy-esque game show announcer voice.

"'NOOOOOOOOOOOTHING'S Too Petty To Tell Me!!!!!!'"

She looked at me quizzically.

"You wanna know the rules? Very simple: THERE IS NOTHING TOO PETTY TO TELL ME! So go ahead, tell me everything you hate about me. Everything you loathe, abhor, detest, deplore, and despise. Shit, everything you even mildly dislike. What irks you the most about me?"

"I don't understand."

"Don't worry, I won't get mad. I want to know. Now. This is actually a great exercise. You have carte blanche. Tell me everything. The more, the better. It will make me a better man. Us, a better couple."

"Uh…"

"For instance…I know I might drink too much for your liking, and maybe you hate my choice of footwear. Or how rarely I shave. I know you hate the stubble scratching your cheeks when we kiss. But what else? How I steal your shampoo? Or clog up your DVR with The Wire? Please hit me where it should hurt. I'd like to know."

Miriam backed off.

"I can't do this." She nervously laughed as she began methodically taking off her shoes.

"Oh, yes you can. We both can."

"Then you go first. Uh…do me."

"'Do me.' Haven't heard that in a while, but are you sure?"

"Go ahead. You know I'm better at following than leading."

"That's true. Fair enough. Well you…"

I looked Miriam up and down. Closed my eyes. Exhaled. Then, let 'er rip.

"You start something but never finish it. Diets, exercise programs, books, DVDs you've rented, hobbies, it doesn't matter."

Around the apartment, a smattering of Miriam's previous hobbies lay about, never dealt with, some never taken out of the box: watercolors, knitting, her yoga mat. A Netflix for Annie Hall had been sitting in the same spot for months.

"You think all your ex-boyfriends are still your buddies. Little secret: they aren't. They are still in love with you. They're just sitting around waiting, pining, hoping you'll either realize you were stupid to have dumped them or that you will one day simply fall back into their arms if they stay in close enough proximity. Like that pathetic gap-toothed realtor idiot, Skip."

"Chip." She corrected me.

On a bookshelf, there were still pics of Miriam with some of exes. That always annoyed me. Then again, I still had nude pics of some of my exes saved in iPhoto. But, at least I had the dignity not to publicly display them.

"You don't eliminate all the hair from your body. Even the tiny blonde forearm and cheek hairs that can only be noticed if the sun shines bright at just the right angle and I have my eyes mere centimeters from the skin surface. Why don't you wax that while you're getting the Brazilian? You know you're getting a slight mustache too."

Miriam self-consciously touched her upper lip.

"You always expect me to cure your boredom. To come up with something exciting to do. I'm not a circus clown or a court jester."

I grabbed Miriam's hands.

"You have disgusting finger and toenails from biting them when you're nervous. You should get more pedis and manis."

I rubbed her arms.

"And you don't lotion your body enough. Your skin gets rough at times. That's acceptable for a man or maybe even a lesbian, but not a dainty lady."

I thought some more. This was fun.

"What else? Hmmm…you're not intellectually curious enough, you are incredibly forgetful, and you hold stuff in."

Miriam was looking more and more confused.

"You think Oprah is God and structure your life philosophies around her show topics."

Miriam softly responded, "All…girls do that."

I smiled, she was right. This was 2006 remember.

"Fair enough, I'll strike that one from the record!"

I pointed at an astrology poster on the wall, a book of horoscopes, and the dreamcatcher necklace she currently wore.

"You believe in the hokum of astrology and dream interpretation."

She touched the necklace hanging between her cleavage.

"And, perhaps worst of all, you allow your parents to control your life."

I touched Miriam on the shoulder and finally exhaled, smiling.

"I guess that's it, Mir."

She remained quiet, taking it all in.

"You know, that felt really good. Now you go. I can't wait to hear what you have for me. I bet it'll be hilarious."

Miriam looked at me, hyperventilating.

"W-w-wait. Devin, you actually think all those terrible things about me?"

I shrugged. "What? It's no big deal. Nobody's perfect."

She began to pant.

"That person sounds terrible. That person…is…me."

"Well…yeah. That's the point."

Miriam began breathing even heavier, freaking out, biting her fingernails, losing her mind.

"Why, why would any one date that person?!"

"You know…"

A single tear rolled down Miriam's cheek.

"You're right…"

More tears started flowing.

"…I don't think I do want to date that person."

She began bawling.

"You're not who I'm looking for."

Howling.

I put my shoes on, opened the door and grabbed my Nerf hoop off it, and turned back toward her, but not before noting:

"I also hate how much you cry."

I walked out of her apartment and never came back.

📍 **Drunx Pub** (w. 52nd St. and Eleventh Ave.) | 3:38 AM

chapter fifteen
WHY IS A SINGLE MAN'S LIFE A BOOZETRAP?

"Les, that's what this decade of being a single man has taught me. All the successes, all the failures, all the fun, and even a little misery, it was necessary. Necessary to teach me what I've been looking for."

Cheryl looked at me.

"You think you finally know, smart guy?"

"Yes, I think I do."

"*To* do? Or *you* do?"

Erin looked disgusted by our little flirtation.

"You're really proud of that story? Ugh."

She got up from her seat and left.

"Where's she going? Should I follow her?" Les wondered.

Cheryl and I nodded and Les stood to chase after her, grabbing his dump box. I looked at Cheryl.

"Yeah, I guess Erin was right. Passive aggression does suck but active aggression is just..."

Cheryl laughed hard.

"Hilarious? Poor girl."

"Erin or Miriam?"

Cheryl considered it. "Both."

"Well, you know my past was important for making me who I am. If I wasn't an aggressive dick to Miriam, I might not be here right now."

"Doing what?"

"Being a sweetie to you."

I raised my eyebrows. But Cheryl just rolled her eyes at me.

"But do you get my point? What I've been trying to explain to Les all night long. That there's so many people in this world that there's nothing wrong with being picky as you try to find what you're actually looking for."

"It seems you sure weren't picky in your past. So what do Devin Satyr's career stats look like, huh?"

I thought about it.

"Enough."

She was testing me.

"I'm sure."

She scanned the room, suddenly a little distant. I tried to reel her back in.

"I'm sorry…I used to suffer from The Coolidge Effect. Do you know about that?"

* * *

One day back in 1928 or so, President Calvin and Mrs. Coolidge were being given a tour of a farm in Idaho or Iowa or some piece of shit town that was as boring then as it is now. First Lady Grace Coolidge was, of course, immaculately dressed, whatever immaculately dressed could possibly mean back in an era when bustles were still *de rigueur* and indoor plumbing didn't even exist in the White House.

She was led through the farm grounds, stepping over horse shit and pig shit and, yes, bull shit, and ultimately chicken shit in a chicken coop as some hick farmer in dusty overalls showed her his digs. Now surrounding Mrs. Coolidge and Farmer Fred were numerous press men in suits, probably with that index card that says "PRESS" in their hat brim, taking notes on their steno pads, ready to write the world's greatest headline should the First Lady actually step in the chicken shit.

GRACE'S SLICK SHIT STEP

A few piles of chicken shit back, The President trailed behind, looking at the same chickens squawking all around him, as his Secret Service Men walked nearby.

Farmer Fred would point at this and that, explaining:

"We's gotta' about five-hun'erd 'er so chick'uns here...producin' several hun'erd t'ousand eggs for America."

The First Lady would nod appreciatively. The press would eagerly scribble some notes. Same old shit.

"Our eggs'll g'out ta grocers in e'ry county in this state, and s'veral grocers in ad-jerning states."

As they kept walking, the farmer showing off his hens, the group approached a large, proud rooster. One giant cock. One giant cock copulating furiously with a tiny hen.

"'Dat der' busy cock, Mrs. Coo'ledge, is Don Juan."

Mrs. Coolidge looked surprised at Don Juan's behavior, though she played it off by asking a question she thought pertinent to the chicken trade.

"How often does he...do *that*?"

Farmer Fred got a coy smile on his grizzled face.

"Less juss say, he works very hard for a livin'."

The press snickered, journalists have always been somewhat lewd, but Mrs. Coolidge was still unsure what exactly she was being told.

"Well how hard?"

"Fackt a' da' matter, ma'am, he's called to 'service' dozens a' times a day. 366 days a leap year."

"Really? That rooster works that hard? Every single day?!"

"Oh yes'm. Bar'ly sleeps, ma'am."

Mrs. Coolidge histrionically touched her décolletage, as if about to go faint from shock.

"Well could a gal imagine a man like that!"

Mrs. Coolidge looked over her shoulder and back toward her husband.

"Boys, be sure to mention that to the President!"

The press laughed hard just as The President finally caught up to them all.

"Dozens of times per day? Really?"

The First Lady was surprised Silent Cal had overhead her, but she nodded affirmatively.

"Impressed, Calvin? Think you could keep up?"

Coolidge looked seriously at the farmer.

"Dozens of times per day, hmmmm...

"Yes'r."

"...but always with the same hen?"

The farmer blushed, he really had no choice.

"Oh Gawd no, Mister Presuhdent. A diff'rent hen every single time!"

Now it was the President's turn to smile.

"And, would you please mention *THAT* to the First Lady!"

* * *

"Yeah, well, Coolidge was a shitty president," Erin noted, having returned with Les who had—finally!—ditched his dump box and now only held his DVD copy of *The Godfather*.

"You know he only took office because Harding died," Les added. They both seemed impressed by each other's trivial knowledge. If he'd had any true knowledge, he would have had the foresight to grab the condoms from his dump box too. Now he was really going to have say "fuck sex," even if he had a shot at it.

"So what's your point, Devin?" Cheryl laughed at me, I'd clearly reeled her back in.

"I think what that story illustrates is that variety is the spice of life."

"Or that you can tell Coolidge was a shitty president," Erin noted, "because the only thing ever named after him was an oh-no-shit scientific theory that proposes men like to sleep with lots and lots of women."

"Yeah, Devin, don't you think a committed, monogamous relationship between two people in love offers variety? Novelty? Offers any of the spices of life?" Les smiled conspiratorially at Erin, she was falling for him as he helped her pile on me.

"The only spice that marriage could possibly offer is a little salt. For the wounds."

I made knowing eye contact at Cheryl. Erin pursed her lips at me.

"You're wrong, Devin. It's your life that is the monotonous one: wake up, jerk off, drink up, goof off, hook up, and get down with some random slut."

"How dare you call Cheryl a slut!" I looked at Cheryl, smiling. "Are you going to let your friend get away with that?"

"Cheryl, you know this is just a pick-up game Devin's playing on you. Les told me when we were alone."

I glared at Les as Cheryl absentmindedly wrote something on a cocktail napkin. She finally looked up.

"Huh?"

"Apparently Devin always does this. When he's out and meets a girl he wants to sleep with. He always claims his single days are 'over.' Claims he's found The One. Leads girls on. By the next morning he's had an epiphany about his epiphany and he's magically back to being single."

Les glared at Erin, clearly pissed she'd betrayed his confidence. He'd never learn. But I didn't really care. I didn't really think this particular revelation would affect me.

"I'm not playing any game with Cheryl. I promise. My crazy single days are over."

"Yet you *are* thirty-four years old and here, still in a bar drinking with a bunch of drunk girls at four in the morning."

"Yeah? So?"

Erin looked at me like I was a moron.

"That's all the proof I need that you're still a single man."

"How's that?"

"Drinking leads to trouble and bad decisions and, it's like, remember that game *Mousetrap*?"

Cheryl perked up and affected a commercial announcer voice, imitating the 1980s commercial.

"'Just turn the crank, and snap the plank, and boot the ball right down the chute! Now watch it roll, and hit the pole, knock the ball into the rubadub-tub!'"

"That's right, Cher'. A night out drinking, for a single creep like Devin, is nothing but a Boozetrap."

"BOOZETRAP"

Cartoonish jingle music plays.

INT. BAR - NIGHT

        COMMERCIAL ANNOUNCER (V.O.)
    Boozetrap, I guarantee, it's the craziest shit you'll ever see!

Devin, moving rigidly like a GAME PIECE, scoots into a bar whose floor has different colored squares making it resemble a BOARD GAME.

        COMMERCIAL ANNOUNCER (V.O.)
           (CONT'D)
    Just enter the bar...

The bartender slides Devin a mason JAR of bourbon.

        COMMERCIAL ANNOUNCER (V.O.)
           (CONT'D)
    And grab the jar.

He slams the drink.

        COMMERCIAL ANNOUNCER (V.O.)
           (CONT'D)
    Now drink the booze.

Devin's eyes become instantly glassy as a

SKANKY GIRL approaches him.

>   COMMERCIAL ANNOUNCER (V.O.)
>   (CONT'D)
>   Here comes the flooze!

The skanky floozy smiles at the clearly wasted Devin.

>   COMMERCIAL   ANNOUNCER   (V.O.)
>   (CONT'D)
>   She tries to flirt.

Devin smiles back, wobbling in his seat.

>   COMMERCIAL ANNOUNCER (V.O.)
>   (CONT'D)
>   You paw her skirt.

Devin stands and the skank grabs his hand.

>   SKANK
>   Let's go to my house.

>   Devin
>   Will ya take off your blouse?

The skank starts dragging Devin away.

>   SKANK
>   But of course, that sounds nice.

                    Devin
        Good, let's go, but first a slice.

INT. PIZZERIA

The skank and Devin sit drunkenly eating slices of pizza.

                    Devin
        It sure is greasy.

                    SKANK
        If you're hard I'm easy.

INT. SKANK'S APARTMENT - LIVING ROOM

In the dark, the skank and Devin strip each other naked.

              COMMERCIAL ANNOUNCER (V.O.)
        Back at her pad, she gets bad.

The skank drags Devin to the bedroom.

INT. SKANK'S APARTMENT - BEDROOM

The lights are on.
              COMMERCIAL ANNOUNCER (V.O.)
        In the bedroom, now let's *vroom vroom*.

The skank tosses a naked Devin onto her bed.

She grabs a condom.

> SKANK
> Time to go, I got the rubber.

The skank rips of her shirt, now naked... and fat.

> Devin
> Oh my God, is that some blubber?!

The skank dives on top of Devin and they begin fucking.

> COMMERCIAL ANNOUNCER (V.O.)
> Too late, the trap is set, here comes the net.

A giant plastic net (a la *Mousetrap*) falls over the bed housing the skank and Devin.

FROM ABOVE, two SEVEN-YEAR-OLDS look down, they have been playing this "board game."

> SEVEN-YEAR-OLDS
> YOU LOOOOOOOSE!

> COMMERCIAL ANNOUNCER (V.O.)
> YOWCH! Boozetrap, I guarantee, it's the craziest shit you'll ever see!

FADE OUT.

"I would play that!" I exclaimed.

"Game night!" Cheryl noted, putting her arm around me.

"You're both playing that game right now!" Erin wailed at us.

Even though I could have buried Erin at this point in the night, I decided to show her some sincerity for once.

"Erin, you're right. I did play that game. Most of my adult life."

"And that's just what's happening tonight…"

"You're drinking here too, Erin."

"Women have better self-control. And…"

Erin looked at Cheryl, then Les.

"Anyway, if Cheryl hadn't dragged me out tonight I would've been sitting home crying by myself. And I wouldn't have met such a great guy."

"Who? That 'alpha male' loser whose number you got?" I asked, fucking around with her.

Erin smiled warmly.

"No. Lesley."

She put her hand on his.

"Think what you must, Erin, but I can assure you, I am done with my Boozetrap days."

"Then prove it." Erin leaned right into my face.

"How can I possibly prove something like that?"

Erin smiled cunningly.

"By not having a one-night stand with Cheryl tonight."

lesson number ten

DEVIN'S FINAL LESSON

"As I said, I will block your cock so hard," Erin cackled, looking at Lesley who joined her in laughing.

"Be my guest…"

"Erin, let's go to the bathroom and let these guys finish their discussion."

As Cheryl escorted Erin off to the bathroom, she handed me the cocktail napkin she'd be scribbling on.

"Her number?" Les wondered.

"Not quite."

I turned it toward him, revealing a dead accurate portrait she had sketched of me.

"She's talented, huh?"

"Not like the floozies you usually one-night stand. Though I'm not sure how you're going to get out of this one. Or *into* that one."

I casually took out my iPhone. Its battery life was now down to 5%.

"You've never used online dating, have you?"

I pulled up an app called Flakr.

"I'd thought about it, but even in my most desperate times, I could never pull the trigger."

"Why?"

"I mean…what if I joined and had no success? Or, worse, *had* success? The rest of my life I'd be stuck answering those 'How'dja guys meet?' questions with total avoidance. I've never understood those couples that proudly appear in Match.com and eHarmony commercials giving their testimonials. How embarrassing."

"I guess love does indeed make you do stupid things."

"Yeah. Like reveal you could only meet your partner online!"

I looked at Les.

"What, you think it's only for dorks?"

"Uh…"

"Well, you're right. But you know, the thing about dorks is… they're usually smart."

"Don't I know it."

"Think about it: if you wanted to go to the best Greek restaurant in the city would you just stumble around a neighborhood until you found a decent gyro? If you wanted to find the best scotch bar in Soho would you just go to one street corner and pray that bar was there? If you wanted to see a great movie would you blindly walk into any theater and hope for the best?"

Les shook his head no.

"So why do men seem content to stumble around life hoping they'll meet the perfect woman for them?"

I pointed around Drunx at all the pathetic men still remaining in the room and the few imperfect women left too.

"Going to the same lame bars, the same lame places, the same lame crowds, crawling around the same lame neighborhoods, and consistently failing with their same lame lameness?"

"Lame sameness."

"Have you ever picked up a woman at Drunx?"

"I guess Erin would be my first."

"And you didn't even meet her at Drunx!"

"It's statistically improbable I *haven't* met a girl at Drunx. Law of averages, you know? Yet I haven't."

"The law of averages is one bad law."

"My dating life is surely worse than the standard deviation. Then again, your dating life is standardly deviant."

"My point is, this way of looking for single women may have flown back in 1950. 1995 even, but now, why not use the tools technology has given us?"

"Yeah?"

"For the first time in the history of the world, I can find *the* one girl in the world perfect for me. She may be in Israel, or China, or fucking New Jersey, but I can find her!"

I pulled up Flakr. The dating app for people who don't *do* online dating.

"I've seen the ads on the subway," Les noted.

I started searching through member profiles, adding certain key words to constantly refine my search.

"I used to think I wanted leggy blondes with big fake tits, voracious sexual appetites, and meager minds."

I flicked through profiles. You could tell all you needed to know about these women simply from their duck-faced avatars and screennames (lilcutey1985, bombshellblonde, lEgGyLaDie, etc).

"I can't believe so many hot women are doing internet dating. They're surely fakes, right?"

"Maybe."

"Set up by companies like Coke and FedEx just to get naive fools like me to click."

"Well, we do have our most committed relationships with corporations nowadays, but still…"

"They must be fakes."

"It's funny, Les, girls claim the media and, yes, commercials give them unfair standards to live up to. But, the media hurts us guys too. They make us think we have to date these kinds of women. I mean, that's who rich guys and celebrities date. These are the kinds of women portrayed in movies and on television. The ones splashed on magazine covers. But, you know, I've finally learned, I don't actually like those kinds of women."

Aaron Goldfarb

"But 'those' kinds of women are who you've always dated."

"I know. And I was wrong too. Hair color, skin tone, breast size, height? Irrelevant qualities."

"You truly believe that?"

"Guys that care about blondeness or tit size are narcissists. They don't care about the girl. They only care about how *they* will look with that girl standing next to them. You remember Amanda?"

"Of course…"

"I always dreamed of dating a tall chick like her."

Amanda was a blonde with fake tits who stood six-foot flat in flats. She truly did look like a model or an actress. Asian tourists would even take pictures of her as she walked by.

"I was always envious when I'd see an average man enter a bar with a statuesque gal on his arm. It didn't even seem to matter how attractive the woman was. I'd see the couple and think, 'Now that man must have something going on!' It looked so confident, sexy, powerful to have a giant beauty at your side. I wanted to be that kind of man."

"Well you were."

"And it sucked."

"I thought you loved it?"

"Sure, I got the reactions I wanted, that was great. But, there were other things…"

"Like?"

"Like…in the bedroom."

"I knew you'd have to get one more sex story in before the night ended." Les couldn't help but laugh at my ridiculousness.

"In missionary I felt like a little ant trying to stay balanced atop a giant hill of soil, no place to dig in my toes or knees for traction. I couldn't throw her legs over my shoulders because it felt as if two giant scissor blades were about to come together to lop my head off. Doggy-style she'd be on all fours and her ass would be up near my chin. The only position that kind of worked was woman-on-top. But I needed binoculars to see her face it was so far from mine!"

I rolled my eyes, mocking him. "Gosh, Devin, that sounds awful."

"It was! Aside from checking 'six-footer' off my checklist."

Les groaned.

"I had to dump her, just like I had to dump..."

"Or *be* dumped."

"Yes. By every girl I've ever dated."

I entered more keywords into my Flakr search.

"You see, Les, after splitting with Miriam, I've spent these last couple years, well, completing my sexual checklist sure, but, more importantly, honing in on what *exactly* it is I want. Figuring out why I was a flake, what was wrong for me, and *who* was right."

As I entered more search terms, less and less profiles appeared on my screen.

"I soon realized what I wanted. What I *needed*. A slight bohemian, sure. She might have a normal job, but a slightly quirky one, advertising, blogger, publishing, whatever. She has more artistic ambitions though."

We watched the women whittling down in my search.

"On the weekends she drags me to weird rock shows in Brooklyn even though I hate live music. We drink PBR in a can and hang with hipsters."

"You? And *hipsters*?"

"You know, Les, they're not so bad. I'm not sure why everyone hates on them so much. They like good food, good drink, good entertainment, and rarely shaving. What exactly is wrong with that?"

Less and...

"She's a big bookworm, but not too big into making pop cultural references since I'd have no idea what she's talking about."

...less and....

"She's not a sports fan but she doesn't care that I am."

"That's more important than girls realize."

"She's not political or religious. Liberal, conservative, anarchist, Communist, Fascist, Jewish, Christian, Buddhist, Satan worshipper...*any* belief is too much for me."

Only ATHEIST and NON-VOTER girls remained on Flaker.

"She drinks. Likes sex. Laid back. *But* ambitious..."

"She's an oxymoron!"

"She has hobbies: drawing, sewing, maybe even surfing in the Rockaways. So few girls seem to have legitimate interests outside of watching *True Blood* and shopping."

I entered some final search terms.

"She champions my dreams. No matter how foolish they are. Even if I want to pursue stupid ones like Beer Muscles or the Dick & Pussy Insurers. And I may indeed pursue that one!"

Les laughed as I entered one final search term.

"And, most importantly of all, she likes to laugh. A *LOT*."

Almost on cue, we heard the sounds of hearty laughter in the back recesses of Drunx. Les immediately froze like a statue like I knew he would.

"No."

I held up my iPhone so Les could see, illuminating his face with a phone spotlight for the first time all evening.

"No!"

Les shook his head in shock, in pure disbelief.

Only one girl on Flakr fit all of my criteria and only one girl's profile remained on my iPhone screen. Still laughing, Cheryl walked up and kissed me passionately on the lips. Like a blackjack dealer, I flipped my iPhone onto the table.

"So I guess it's time to delete my profile, huh, Sweetie?"

The iPhone spun slowly like a top, Cheryl's Flakr profile displayed.

"You two?!"

If Les sat stupefied, Erin appeared mortified.

"You date this...*scumbag*, Cher?"

The iPhone finally stopped spinning, pointing like a bottle at Cheryl and me, before it finally went black, its batteries finally dead.

"Now now, Erin. She's been dating this scumbag for the last six months. But don't worry—I *won't* break my promise to you. I won't have a one-night stand with her this evening."

"Tonight will be about, what? Our hundredth-night stand or so…"

"But who's counting?"

Cheryl smiled and sat down on my lap.

"I love you, Sweetie"

"I love you too."

Cheryl looked at Erin and Les, explaining: "We just started saying 'it' today."

"You're no longer a single man, Devin?"

"I guess I'm not. So that would be the fifth and final reason to ever say 'Fuck sex.' Because you're with someone. Monogamously. Forever."

Cheryl rubbed my head, laughing.

Les racked his brain, like he was trying to understand the climax of a movie with a surprise ending. I was Keyser Söze in love.

"He's not a scumbag either, Erin. He's the best, most perfect man I've ever known."

"But, Cheryl, what about his sordid past? What about all of his bullshit?!"

Erin was almost pleading with Cheryl.

"We share everything with each other. I've never met such an honest guy."

"Hey! I know about her sordid past too! That Brooklyn Heights story is absurd. Do you know *that* one?"

I squeezed Cheryl's waist as she playfully punched me.

"If you're gonna live a life, you have to have a past," Cheryl noted.

Les looked quickly at Erin, then me.

"Why didn't you tell—?"

"You've been too busy, pal. With Jenn and everything."

Erin quickly looked at Les, then Cheryl.

"Why didn't you mention—?"

"You've been too caught up in your own stuff with Joe."

Les finally understood everything.

"Your guide? It was never for me…"

Everyone was shooed outside the bar, it now reading 4:27 AM on our smartphones. With the sun rising over the East River and Midtown skyline, and everyone yawning, perhaps looking for some ill-advised street meat to eat, Erin and Les gathered around Cheryl and me.

"So that's how easy it is, Les. To go from a perpetually single man to dating the woman of your dreams. You don't need gimmicks."

I thought of the alpha males.

"Or Machiavellian cruelty."

Les nodded.

"You don't need wealth, money, power, or even sex appeal."

"Well good! I don't have any of those things."

Erin rubbed Les's back. "That's not true."

"And you don't even need to get her wasted. Though that does occasionally help."

Cheryl smiled at me.

"You just need confidence."

I looked Les in the eyes.

"Being yourself."

I put my hands on his shoulders.

"Being, not a nice guy, but a *good* guy."

Erin now had her arm around Les's lower back.

"And, OK, I lied…perhaps a little luck too. Hey, it's a complex world."

Cheryl and I departed, walking east across 52nd Street toward the rising sun and Cheryl's apartment.

"Do you think our friends will get together tonight, Sweetie?"

Once the bars closed, you never knew who would head back home, back wherever, back to bed, back to A bed, with whatever single man, or single woman, he or she, or *me*, they had met that very evening. Anything was possible and that's what made this city so great.

"Yeah, maybe. I still remember the first night we got together. Do you?"

continue the story by picking up

THE GUIDE FOR A SINGLE WOMAN

AVAILABLE NOW AT FGPRESS.COM
AND OTHER RETAILERS

chapter one

EVERYTHING HAPPENS FOR A REASON

How did we get here?

You and me.

How did we get—

Look, I know you hate these talks. Fine, get your jokes out. We got here…?

"By a smelly cab."

Nice.

"By a smelly cab with a smelly driver who took us to this smelly bar."

Funny. Well your tip also stunk. Yeah, I saw. That was a poor tip even converted to rupees.

But, seriously, how did we get here?

I wish you'd just tell me things, Sweetie. Then, I wouldn't need to piece together your backstory. Either through Google stalking or those rare bits you're actually willing to share. Other bits suppressed either 'cause you're hiding something…or simply 'cause you claim the details are too boring.

They're not boring to me. Nothing about you is boring to me.

Of course I've Googled you!

Let's see…you were born in Kansas City in 1979 and grew up there until you left in 1996. You went to college up here. You were raised by distant parents, but, despite that, you surely had a better childhood than 99% of all people in the world today. Mine was probably better than 99.9%. But you already know my bits and pieces. All of them.

I was born at Mass General and grew up in the Rhode Island suburbs where I went to a small enough school I could be both valedictorian and popular. Invited to cool parties, yet win science fairs. Where I could be All-Conference in basketball and homecoming queen. (You've seen the pictures. I looked ridiculous getting that sash put over my sweaty jersey.) My life as a kid was pretty darn perfect. A prostate cancer scare for Dad, my cat Charcoal accidentally backed over by Mom's station wagon, sure, but those were just bumps in the road of my charmed childhood.

So should we even begin with you and me? Should you ever start with "you and me"?

Instead, let's start with your dad. Scott, right? What if he'd never met your mother? Meryl, correct? Pretty name. I hope to meet them someday.

What if your dad had been infertile? Or your mom barren? What if you'd been given up for adoption? Or…terminated? Your parents were struggling when you were born, right? What if they had gotten divorced before you'd even been conceived… instead of just four years later?

We could go back to your Grandfather Jay. What if he'd died in Korea? Or your great-grandfather, Saul. OK, so I might have played around on Ancestry.com. But, what if Saul had been turned away at Ellis Island, sent back to Poland? What if he'd died of polio? What if Jonas Salk had never been born? Then we might not be here, you and me.

What if you had died in that car accident at nine? Your mom's minivan flips on the highway yet you all just walk away? Nothing more than a few bruises and a sizable settlement from Toyota?

What if your mother had spent that settlement on a Disneyland vacation instead of using it to move you into a nicer school district? (When are you going to take me back to visit?) What if your high school sweetheart hadn't gotten that abortion? You say you weren't "sweethearts," but if you get a high school girl pregnant, she's gonna be your sweetheart for the rest of time. Now you'd be watching your sixteen-year-old son play under Friday night lights instead of drinking some Friday night light beers with me.

Yeah, this beer sucks, we really should have gone some place else.

Luckily for us, I guess, the pregnancy was terminated and your sweetheart became your sweet-not and now you're my Sweetie.

What if NYU had given you a scholarship? You'd have attended.

What if you'd followed your friends to that crappy state school? Four years of partying and now you'd live in St. Louis or Dallas. You'd wear golf shirts and khakis every day of your life.

What if you'd been a frat boy? You might be married to some airhead who still sleeps in shorts with Greek letters on the butt.

What if you'd accepted that entry-level job in Chicago? You'd be dating some girl with a thick accent and thick meat on her bones. You might be a Cubs fan. You might be that Steve Bartman guy. You'd be in hiding and I never would have met you.

What if you'd used Match or eHarmony or even JDate? I know you're not Jewish, but non-Jews still like to use it to find hot little Jews like me. OKCupid? OKStupid. But, what if we both didn't use the dating website we did? What if some surely virginal nerd in his Silicon Valley garage hadn't invented that site? What if a VC hadn't given the surely virginal nerd enough funding and he was forced to fold up shop before we ever had a chance to use it? What if just one of us hadn't had the courage to use online dating? Then there'd never be you and me.

Millions, if not billions of things had to happen for you to find yourself here with me at this smelly little pub on Columbus Circle. Even Columbus had to discover America, or wherever this is, for *this* to happen. Manhattan could still be a forest, still owned by Native Americans and never sold for beads, this place where we currently sit.

Another billion, if not trillions of things had to happen for me to find myself here sitting with you.

Did you know I nearly joined Teach for America out of college? Then what? Get accepted, get sent to North Dakota or Hawaii…*or Peru*, and all of the sudden nothing will ever be the same. I'd be dating some vegan hippie who wears Toms on his feet and Tom's under his armpits and goes to Burning Man every single year.

Did you know I was mugged that summer I lived in Bushwick? What if he had killed me? Or scared me so much I moved back home? I nearly did. My mother begged me to.

Did you know I nearly didn't do online dating because I thought the sites would be full of cheap hipsters with bad beards? And, you know, it *was*. For the first seventeen dates I was batting 0.000. No good first dates, certainly no seconds, no hugs, no kisses, no nothing. A lot of free meals at crappy bars… but that was it.

Then, date eighteen: You.

And I was date one for you.

(So you say.)

That sounds even more amazing, more unlikely.

What if you assumed it would only get better from there and decided to go on more dates? Even just to see if other chicks were as easy as me. Maybe you did. Maybe you still are…?

I know you aren't. Don't worry, Sweetie, I was only kidding. But why haven't you deleted your online profile? You could use that $14.99 a month to buy me a nice cocktail tonight.

Don't worry. I know you have your reasons.

I know you think this is silly.

I know you don't believe everything happens for a reason.

You believe in strategy, not fate.

You believe you seduced me using brilliant strategy. You did this and then that which then caused me to do that and then this.

You think years of "experience," trial and error, and some impeccable strategy brought you to a point where I was just another girl in the layup line of taking New York City girls to bed. If you only knew, Sweetie.

You believe in strategy and sex.

I believe in fate and love.

We were meant to be together.

You didn't need to use strategy.

How could it not be fate when I've just shown you how many thing had to perfectly happen for us to get to this point? I was always meant to meet you and sleep with you and be with you and love you.

Then again, you being a charming and witty guy who uses strategy was meant to be too. The strategy was secondary, though, just a part of our fate.

Me and you. You and me? It was meant to be. It was fate that got us to the point where I will now be the first to say it, six months into our relationship:

"I love you."

That's nice to hear back. I know you love me. You say it whenever you're drunk. But that doesn't count. This does and that just did.

I love you, Sweetie.

Now you're embarrassed. I know you don't like when I get like this.

But I do love you so so much.

Oooh…that's Erin, she's finally out of work.

OK, Sweetie, goodbye. Will I see you later tonight?

Of course I will. I'll see you every tonight for the rest of my nights.

ACKNOWLEDGMENTS

I would like to thank Brad Feld, Dane McDonald, and the team at FG Press for giving me this incredible opportunity. This includes Sandy Grason, Kevin Kane, Eugene Wan, and Dave Heal. I would like to thank the great Craig T. Wood for spurring the idea for these works and Phil Simon for setting me up with FG Press. And I would like to thank Betsy for now giving me *The Guide for a Married Man*.

ABOUT THE AUTHOR

Aaron Goldfarb is the author of *How to Fail: The Self-Hurt Guide*, the 2010 satirical novel that has sold over 100,000 copies. Aaron was born in Manhattan, raised in Oklahoma City, and attended Syracuse University's Newhouse School. In addition to *How to Fail*, Aaron has a short story collection about "the sexes, sex, and sexiness in New York," *The Cheat Sheet* (2011), as well as a book of his collected drinking essays, *Drunk Drinking* (2012). A noted craft beer and spirits expert, Aaron writes about those subjects and more on a weekly basis for *Esquire*. He is also a frequent contributor to *Playboy*, MTV, and *Draft Magazine* and currently has several film and television projects in various stages of development. He lives in New York City and can be contacted via email aaron@aarongoldfarb.com or on Twitter @aarongoldfarb.

ABOUT FG PRESS

Thank you for supporting the future of publishing! We are FG Press, a small group of entrepreneurs crazy enough to think that we can change the world of publishing. We do this by putting our authors first, and by creating a community of involvement between authors, editors, designers, and readers.

FG Press was founded in late 2013 by the team at Foundry Group. As venture capitalists and authors, we believe there is a clear path of innovation away from the current publishing model—one that is defined by one-sided royalty splits, cumbersome bureaucracy, poor transparency, and ineffective support—to one that can better serve authors and readers.

Welcome to the family. Send us an email (info@fgpress.com) to let us know how we're doing and we'll send you something awesome in return (like a coupon code for another one of our titles).

Join the conversation amongst our authors and readers in The Parlour at parlour.fgpress.com and follow us on Twitter and Facebook. Thank you!

CPSIA information can be obtained at www.ICGtesting.com
Printed in the USA
BVOW02s1005050115

381964BV00001B/5/P